NOTES FROM THE END OF THE WORLD

Vol. 1: Cindy's Story

DONNA BURGESS

Notes from the End of the World
Vol. 1
ISBN: 978-0692300251
First Edition
Published by Naked Snake Press
©2014 Donna Burgess
Cover illustration © 2023 Donna Burgess

This book is a work of fiction. Names, characters, businesses, places, events, locales, and incidents are either the products of the author's imagination or used in a fictitious manner. Any resemblance to actual persons, living or dead, or events is coincidental.

Published by Naked Snake Press, Pawleys Island, SC
ISBN: 978-0692300251

A Note to Our Valued Readers:

As an independent author, your support means the world to me. If you enjoyed this journey into my imagination, please consider taking a moment to share your thoughts with others. A brief review on Amazon can help immensely to support independent authors like myself. It doesn't have to be long—a few words about what you enjoyed (or could improve) can make a significant difference. Your feedback helps me grow as a writer but also assists fellow readers in discovering new tales that might resonate with them.

Thank you for investing your time in my story, and I look forward to hearing your thoughts.

Donna Burgess, author/owner, Naked Snake Press

This journey is dedicated to you.

MY NAME IS CINDY SCOTT. I'M SIXTEEN YEARS OLD AND I'M GOING TO TELL YOU HOW THE WORLD ENDS...

CHAPTER 1

◆

April 30
Cindy

Maybe I'm stupid for running, but what have I been doing for the last nine months, anyway? Running. I need to run. It's the last thing I have left of my old life. Everything else has been taken—my parents, my friends, my school. My future.

It's warmer now, and my breaths come hot and damp. I found Dad's iPod in his office and now Springsteen blasts into my ears. I wouldn't have listened to Bruce before, but I do now because it reminds me of Dad and Mom. I'd better enjoy it. The battery is showing low.

Sometimes I wonder what happened to Bruce. And Zac Efron and the incredibly hot guy from Vampire Diaries. Are they dead? Are they ...changed? Are they running around a doomed neighborhood pretending life is still normal, too?

Common logic indicates that I need to be able to hear them coming. Shamblers are slow, but they can be surprising. Especially when they move in droves. But I know them by their smell. Death has this distinctive stink. It floats up like rancid garbage. It smells...feverish. And no matter how much I smell it, I never grow used to it.

During the brief hours when the Internet and electricity were on, Nick and I printed out a map of Sawgrass Flats from Google Earth and traced our running route. We then determined where we could strategically place weapons. Just in case.

Behind Mr. Law's house, we left a pair of hedge trimmers. A block over, we stood a short, sharp spade next to Mrs. Billings' garage. Another block farther along, we left one of my softball bats behind the rose bushes at Mr. David's and Mr. Howard's elegant cottage. David was meticulous over those roses. There's nothing left but a tangle of thorny vines now. I'd heard that David had to kill Howard. After that, he vanished. I assumed he killed himself, too. He always said he couldn't get along without Howard.

I'm quick enough to sprint between weapons, if necessary. I haven't had to yet, but luck has this dumb way of running out, doesn't it?

The morning sun is bright and dew glistens like shards of glass on forgotten lawns. A little dog peers at me from behind a thick oak tree. He trots along with me, keeping up but staying back, timid of humans now. When I turn, he darts away.

Farther ahead, I step over the remains of another little pooch that's been dead for over a week. Every time I run, my eyes are drawn to it. Maybe on a subconscious level, I'm trying to see how it changes, and how decay *really* works. It's an amazing thing, rot. Does it work its way in from the outside or is it the other way around?

How I've always loved my neighborhood. It's the only place I've ever known. The only place I've ever lived. I love the big oak trees that line the curving roads. Kids at school used to say I live in a "richy" neighborhood. Maybe so, but it no longer matters. Who's rich now? The ones who have food? The ones who still have someone to love and to love them back?

The people in the Flats were like family, seeing each other every day, coming and going. A wave or a nod or a quick chat about school or track or soccer. The houses are nothing but caves now. Big, empty, brick caves. Normally, everyone would've had the lawns decorated for Halloween. Neat Halloween trees and Jack-o-lanterns. Mr. Graves (of all people) would've set up a mock cemetery in his front yard, complete with Styrofoam tombstones, creepy gauze cobwebs hanging from the trees, and a couple of hands plunging upward from the earth.

Ironic.

By Halloween last year, the N-Virus was beginning to wrap its stinking fingers around the heart of Palmdale. Mr. Graves had decorated anyway, but later at the community Christmas pow-wow, he mentioned how he regretted it. Mrs.

Graves had turned by January and went to the Pastures soon after.

I pass the Jensen's place—the prettiest home in the Flats. Like many of the other homes, their front door sports a messy red spray-painted "CLEARED." The windows above the porch are broken out. Someone else must be around, lying low. Maybe watching me as I pass. Switching off my music, I jog along, even more watchful now, because sometimes the living are worse than the dead. Guardsmen, police, soldiers and scavengers are a rare sight lately, but still, it's best to take no chances. People you could trust a year ago are the ones you now have to avoid at all costs. They're the ones with the guns, so they're the ones with the power.

I stop, bend at the waist and suck clean, cool air. Another. And here it is—that smell. That stink I've come to know so well.

Straightening up, I slowly turn and look around. To the right, I spot the Shambler. He might've been somewhere around middle-aged if he'd lived. He's wearing stained pajama pants, no shirt, and no shoes. His gray hair sticks out from his head like a frizzy halo. The bones of his chest glint through the rotten, moss-colored tatters of flesh.

I learned quickly I could determine how long a Shambler's been a Shambler by the size of its smile. The dead have these perpetual smiles created by the lack of lips. Lips are the first things to go after the virus takes hold. The hunger grows so strong, that they just eat them off.

I've seen it firsthand, that nightmarish, desperate hunger.

I dart to the left and double back toward the Jensen's place. Despite the lack of decent food, I'm quick. But the Shamblers are quick, too, and this one is on me in an instant, the stink of his breath wafting up from behind. He grabs my ponytail, but his grip is no good because the pads of his fingers are gone. I slip away as his teeth click together loudly, a near miss at the side of my throat.

I'd left a short-handled pickaxe near the Jensen's back patio, but it's so far away. But I need to get there before Mr. Pajama Pants has me for lunch.

I leap over the little garden wagon, turn, and shove it back toward the Shambler. He stumbles, growling loudly, but it only slows him down a step, maybe not even that.

"Shit," I mutter. The pickaxe is there, ten feet away, but suddenly I'm like some dumbass chick from a horror movie and I fall on my face. Mr. Pajama Pants takes advantage of this and snatches at my flailing leg. Rolling over, I kick straight out, connecting with what was left of his face. It's like kicking a cardboard box; there's no weight there, nothing of substance. But the kick is good enough. As I mentioned, I was a soccer player before the end of the world and my kicks aren't weak.

The Shambler's head flies back, his neck cracking audibly. I might've cringed, but I've heard worse in the past year.

Either way, it gives me the time I need to get to that pickaxe.

I grab it up and spin back toward my friendly neighborhood Shambler. Steeling myself (isn't that a comic book line), I raise the pickaxe, ready.

Mr. Pajama Pants lunges at me, his stupid mouth wide open, his teeth looking huge without lips to frame them. I wait for the exact instant and then plunge the pointed blade of the axe forward. It sinks into his eye—all the way in. The eyeball pops like an old tomato and splatters on my face and hands. I shove it harder and he stops moving altogether. The smell of rancid blood fills my nostrils and I turn my face away, searching for a clean breath.

If you've seen pretty much any zombie movie, you know you need to aim for the head. The brain has to be destroyed. That's rule number one. If you can't remember that one, you're not going to get very far.

Pajama Pants thrusts his arms at me one last time and then sinks to his knees. He's done and I'm done with him. I let go of the axe and plant my foot in his chest, shoving him backward. Then I step over him, plug my earbuds back into my ears, and start running again. Nick's usually with me, so of course, the day he's not is the day I get a visit from a Shambler. Maybe it'll be best to keep it to myself.

CHAPTER 2

Seven months earlier
Cindy

"I saw you checking out his ass," Melissa says, quickening her pace to keep up with me.

"You're not supposed to notice," I tell her.

"Hard not to. You're practically drooling." She falls behind again and I slow, allowing her to catch up. For me, running is as easy as breathing. I've been on the cross-country team for the past two years, and have played soccer since I was eight. Not so much for Melissa, who looks awkward in her heavy jewelry and overly dressy top that is not made for doing much more than shopping.

I'd assumed morning gym class would be a disaster, but that was until I realized Nick Thatcher was also in the class. Now, having to redo my hair and makeup is a reasonable trade-off.

Nick runs easy, his strides long and sure. The lean muscles in the backs of his legs flex and relax, and his auburn hair swings. For gym class, he always wears these incredible red shorts that hug his hiney just right. Watching him makes the forty minutes pass by in a blink.

Of course, watching (as discreetly as possible, by the way) is all I can do. He belongs to Audrey. I'm just the kid-sister, hanging like a shadow in his peripheral vision. He's nice to me because he has to be.

The rest of the day is a blur of boredom. It isn't special, it's just Tuesday. All through lunch, Melissa chatters about some dumb pop singer I've barely heard of. I prefer Indie rock—pop music is just plain dumb. Worse, Melissa's blonder, tanner clone, Eva Adams, tries to set me up with Jake Wylie, who's only forty pounds overweight and has a better set of hooters than even Audrey has. This is the second set-up in a month—Mom set me up with a client's creepy son two weeks ago. She was desperate to get the listing on a big commercial building on the other end of town. The owner's son, Russell, wasn't exactly hot, and what he lacked in looks he made up in obnoxiousness. To make things worse, I called Mom a pimp, only half-kidding, and was grounded from the Internet for two days.

Russell really knew how to make a girl feel good about herself. The first thing he asked, after meeting me and then meeting Audrey was, "How does it feel to be the sister of the hottest chick in your school?"

I should've kicked him in the balls, but instead, I said nothing and faded into the velvet curtains of the Palmdale movie house.

The bad experience with Russell aside, hurting someone's feelings for no better reason than to make a couple of shallow cheerleaders giggle isn't my style. Screw them.

I still have two years to go before getting out of Palmdale. Two long, boring years of listening to the same boring blather from the same boring people every day. Worse, in a year, Nick will be gone to a college a thousand miles away, if he's smart. Seeing Audrey go won't be nearly as bad.

To round out a perfectly shitty day, Audrey complains about dropping me off at the hospital after school, although it's only a couple of miles out of the way.

The first of the infected bursts through the double doors of the E.R. shortly after four p.m. There's no soccer practice on Tuesdays, so I volunteer at Mercy General Hospital.

I think I recognize the guy, but there's no way to be certain. Everything moves too fast—I can't get a proper look at him. Every time the cluster of bodies around him parts enough for me to see, his face contorts into this enraged snarl. That kind of look isn't common in Palmdale. People here don't become enraged. They get miffed, peeved and occasionally, they get pissed off. But enraged? That's about as common as a meteor strike. This is fucking scary, tear-your-face-off anger.

The other thing that hits me, aside from the crazy-person expression, is the color, or lack of color, in his face. It's a shade of gray that can only be associated with death. Living people just don't look like that. Even his eyes hold that same lack of color. They're as pale as the skin on a fish's belly.

Maybe he's a real estate agent or works at the bank. His suit looks expensive despite the condition it's now in—tattered, wrinkled, the sleeve missing from one arm. He's also missing a loafer and his long, skinny legs flail wildly on the gurney. Something dark dots his pant legs like spilled paint.

The stink of roadkill rises from him, filling the narrow entrance corridor. I want to gag, but what does that say about a girl who plans to go to med school?

Two nurses--heavy-set and usually talkative Jolee and the smaller, but equally exuberant Sara, struggle with Mr. Grayface's flying arms. Dr. Jacobs joins the fray and is instantly struck in the side of the head by Grayface's arm. His glasses clatter to the floor, smashing under the wheels of the gurney.

Jolee cries out as Grayface shoves her to the side. She sags against the wall, her bright red hair coming free of the pretty comb she always wears, hiding her horrified face.

Sara makes a valiant attempt to secure both arms, but it's useless. He writhes, shaking her this way and that, until she stumbles backward and falls, her head striking the floor with a dull, sickening thud.

I run to her and help her to her feet, which is no easy task. Poor Sara has the look of someone who is suffering from a concussion as I pull her away from the melee.

"You're in no shape to help them now," I tell her, stating the obvious.

Dr. Jacobs somehow manages to fasten the belts across the man's thrashing legs. Grayface howls and whips his head violently from side to side, saliva, sweat, and blood misting the air.

"Get him a sedative. Now!" Dr. Jacobs barks.

Jolee vanishes down the hallway. A security guard dashes past us and throws himself across the crazy man's torso, forcing him back to the gurney. "Christ! Get those cuffs off my belt and hand them to me," he shouts. He must outweigh Grayface by thirty pounds, but it doesn't matter. Grayface flings him away like he's tossing away a rag doll.

Grayface then snatches Dr. Jacobs by the sleeve of his lab coat and it's all over in an instant. Like a rabid animal, he bites into Dr. Jacobs' forearm. Shaking his head, the madman tears away cloth and flesh. Dr. Jacobs sinks to the floor, blood shooting from his wounded arm toward the ceiling like water escaping a broken hose. His face matches the color of his white coat as he places his hand over the gash, attempting to slow the flow of blood.

Then Dad's here. "Get back, Cindy. Don't come near." He yanks on a pair of latex gloves and rushes to his friend.

Grayface's legs escape the belts. He springs from the gurney and starts toward my dad. Screaming, I rush forward. I don't know what the hell I think I'm going to do. Looking back on it, I realize how stupid that was. It doesn't matter, anyway. The security guard puts a bullet in the man's forehead before he takes another step.

Everything goes quiet. Shock is as contagious as a virus. I can't move. I can't breathe. I just stand there, staring like a dumb kid. I want my dad, but he's already vanished down the hallway with Dr. Jacobs, leaving a wide trail of blood on the floor behind them.

Later, as Dad drives home, both of us are silent and still a little in shock, and it occurs to me that I watched Dr. Jacobs die today. He isn't dead yet, but his fate's sealed. Just like the rest of the world. It's just a question of time. The N-Virus is no longer news, rumors, and things that happen to other people in other cities. It's real.

It's everywhere and there's no hiding from it anymore.

Audrey stands in the doorway of my bedroom as if she's afraid to come in completely, brushing her hair so hard that I wince with every stroke. She always brushed like that—as if she was angry with her own hair. Of course, it doesn't hurt—her hair's gorgeous. Thick and dark, a sharp contrast to my pale blonde locks. My hair's too fine and straight to keep in a proper ponytail. Of course, Audrey's opposite of me in most ways. She always looks good—even when she's ready for bed, dressed in Dad's Duke Blue Devils t-shirt that's at least three sizes too large and a pair of boy shorts. Without makeup, she's still hotter than I can ever imagine being. I have to put on makeup just to look like I'm old enough to drive. I'd come to terms with that a couple of years ago. Audrey's the pretty one and I'm the smart one. At least I have something.

Dad told me once that people lose their looks a lot sooner than they lose their minds. That's good enough for me.

"So, you didn't get anything on you, did you?" Audrey raises one perfectly arched eyebrow. "Blood? Spit? Snot?"

I close my laptop and move it to the desk, then sink on the bed. "No. I didn't get anything on me. But Dr. Jacobs was bitten on the arm."

A flash of sadness crosses Audrey's face, but it's gone before I'm sure I've actually seen it. We'd known Bill Jacobs and his wife Maureen our entire lives. The Jacobs have two sons (who are super-cute, by the way) in college. Dr. Jacobs always had grape Dum-Dums tucked away in the pocket of his lab coat.

"That's too bad." She frowns. "Do you think he'll turn into one of them?"

"I hope not. But Dad says probably. They have him quarantined."

"And they shot the guy in the head?"

"Yeah," I squeeze my eyes shut. This is a time when I wish I could have an instant memory loss button. I'd lose today and never miss it.

"Wow. That was weird." Audrey's not very good at compassion. Once, we had a cat named Felix who was killed by a Doberman that had escaped his kennel. She said the same thing then.

"Mom wants you to quit until this N-Virus thing blows over." She stops brushing her hair, twists it up into a loose bun, then clips it. "I don't understand why you bother with that volunteering stuff, anyway. Why does it matter so much? Helping people, I mean."

I shrug. After today's events, I wonder that myself. "I want to see whether I'm cut out for it. Dad's happy with being a doctor. I think I would be, too. Besides, helping people is what you're supposed to do." Then I smile and add, "If you're normal, that is."

"Who said? People are shit, little sis. You need to do what makes you happy, not what other people expect. Besides, nothing's important enough to risk your own skin. You know, for a brainiac you can be really dumb sometimes." One of her backhanded compliments. This is as good as I'll ever get from my big sister.

"It's what I want."

"Okay," Audrey answers. "You know, being normal is overrated." That's it. She's gone back to her room, across the hall, the door closing behind her.

I sink back down onto the bed, pick up my IPad from the bedside table and switch it on, staring at the screen, not reading. The image of Dr. Jacobs' terrified face refuses to leave my mind. What if that had been Dad? Or me? What then? What'll happen if one of us catches the N-Virus? I'm not sure any of us could function if we lost one. My family is like a car. If we lose a wheel, all of us will be stuck.

Later, Dad pops into my room and sits on the edge of the bed.

"Let's not tell your mother what happened today, okay?" he says. "You know it'll scare her."

I nod. "I know. I'm not sure I would want to, anyway. Talking about it means I have to think about it." I laugh nervously. "I definitely don't want to think about it."

"But it's hard not to, isn't it?" Dad asks. He strokes my hair just as he used to when I was a little girl.

He always seems to know what's going on in my head. We're connected, the two of us. Just like Audrey and Mom are connected.

"I see it every time I close my eyes," I whisper.

"It gets easier, but you never get used to it," he tells me, "but that's part of being a doctor."

CHAPTER 3

September 14
Cindy

The next morning Mom opts for NPR instead of her usual morning jazz. She's an odd one sometimes—she has this impression that relaxing music will give us a good start to our school day. She's done this since Audrey was getting ready for kindergarten, and I was still running around in Pull-Ups. It's never worked with Audrey, as far as anyone could tell, but Mom will never admit it. At least she doesn't rub Geranium oil on our foreheads to help keep us "balanced," like Grandma does when we visit her. Grandma claims to be a practicing witch. Dad tends to agree, but he's only shared that with me. Audrey would blab and Mom would get pissed if they heard him say it.

I've changed my mind. If the four of us are a car, then Dad and I are a bicycle. Does that make any sense?

The rich, smoky scent of coffee fills the air, something I love, although I'm not a big coffee drinker. My friends sip cups of coffee when they hang out at the mall, working so hard to look cool and adult. I just don't care about that. Give me a chocolate shake any day.

Audrey emerges from upstairs looking more prepared for a photo shoot than a Wednesday at Palmdale High School. Dressed in a short, expensive plaid skirt and a Hollister t-shirt that's small enough to fit a toddler, she shoots me a look as she peels a banana. "You're wearing that?"

I have on a perfectly respectable pair of pink Ralph Lauren Bermuda shorts and a white blouse. Besides my Keds are sparkling white.

"Yeah, I'm wearing this," I mutter. "National dress-like-a-hooker day isn't until next week. Didn't you get the memo?"

"Cindy!" Mom cries.

Dad laughs behind his iPad.

"Dyke," Audrey retorts. Mom doesn't say anything to her and I'm not surprised. Mom never calls her out.

I'm terrible at witty comebacks or even the bitchy ones Audrey's so good at dishing out. I'm good for about one a month if that. It doesn't matter. The news starts and Mom turns the radio louder.

"Thompson health officials announced the county is now in a State of Emergency due to the Necro-Mortosis Virus epidemic. Thompson County Director of Health and Human Services, Isaiah Neville, said this week eight more deaths related to the virus has brought the total count inside the county up to eighteen so far."

Audrey starts to say something else, but Dad stops her. "Shhh. Wait."

Audrey doesn't like to be shushed. She pulls a pissed-off face and pours herself a cup of coffee. Smiling, I finish my Honey Bunches.

"The virus has now been reported in all fifty states, resulting in more than 300 confirmed deaths. The number of causalities has reached triple digits in parts of Europe, but those numbers may be higher, given the nature of the disease.

"The risk to both citizens and Healthcare workers is extremely high during an N-Virus outbreak. Apart from Necro-Mortosis contagion from bites, exposure can occur through exposure to bodily fluids such as blood, saliva, mucus, and semen."

"Eww," Audrey says. "Who would want to screw a zombie?"

"Don't be so vulgar, Audrey," Mom tells her.

"In related news," the newscaster goes on, sounding strangely cheerful for such a newscast, "Pro-Life advocates have begun protests in several Southern and Mid-Western states arguing the ethical ramifications of putting down infected victims. More and more areas are moving to a stable system, often adjoining established cemeteries. This system allows the infected victims to remain in safety until their bodies expire naturally."

Mom sits down at the kitchen table next to Dad. Looking worried, she nibbles an overly-toasted half of an English muffin. The sun hits her just right and for a moment, she looks as young as Audrey. Both have that exotic olive skin color and dark hair. I'm fair like Dad, which isn't such a bad thing, aside from the stigma blondes carry. Of course, Mom's good looks come at the hands of Dr. Warner, his little friend Botox, and an open checkbook. She's in real estate, after all. Top sellers can't go around looking like hags.

"The Wood Lawn Cemetery has just purchased the big piece of land adjoining the back side of the property," she says. As a commercial broker, she always knows what new businesses are coming to town. "They will be adding those stables. They're calling it the Pastures. Isn't that strange? The Pastures."

"They're just going to put the dead out in a field to walk around?" I don't like the sound of that. Something about it just bites at me, no pun intended. The idea of dead loved ones just stumbling around in a cow pasture is well... sickening.

"Sounds homey," Dad comments brightly. He takes a sip of coffee and glances over his tablet at me. I read his face. He's thinking about what happened at the hospital yesterday.

"What would you want to do if it were someone you loved?" Mom asks.

"I couldn't bear 'putting them down,' as they call it." I can tell she's thinking about Grandma. She mentioned just the other night bringing Grandma to our house until the epidemic is over, but Grandma's too independent for that.

"We all knew it would come here eventually," Dad says, putting his iPad down. "We can pretend it won't, but it's stupid to fool ourselves. Better to be safe. I want to call a family meeting this evening."

"A family meeting?" Audrey complains, following that with a sarcastic gagging sound.

Dad ignores her. "Don't make plans. Be here for dinner. This means you, Audrey."

"Yippee," she whispers, picking up her car keys and her book bag. "Get your things, if you want a ride."

Somehow, throughout the morning's news and subsequent plans for the dreaded family meeting, I managed to miss the real news of the day. The talk around the school was that Sean McKinley, the "super-hot" star of the Ghost Chronicles had contracted the N-Virus. His smooth, little teenage face graces many a locker around Palmdale High. Frankly, Sean isn't my type. He's way too perfect for me. Boys prettier and more delicate than I am don't interest me very much.

"Did you hear about Sean?" Amy Gerber always calls television stars by their first names as though she knows them personally. Annoying, but I've learned to live with it. We all have our silly little quirks, I suppose. Mom calls them "personality traits," a nicer term for it, I suppose. Either way, later I'll learn how I miss those little quirks.

"No. What's up?" I slide into my desk, flip open my notebook, and pull out my biology homework. Everyone else files in, laughing and chatting leisurely—Mrs. Bell's always late to begin the First Period. Rumor has it she drinks and stays in the girl's bathroom until everyone has cleared out, sucking down cheap wine. I find that hard to believe. She looks more like a vodka drinker.

Amy wraps the end of her straight brown hair around her pencil like it's a curling iron as if it's going to give her straight hair some bounce. Another funny habit, but she's done that since first grade. I love Amy, but she's still such a little kid—she hasn't changed since middle school. She's an only child, spoiled, but then again, every kid in Palmdale is spoiled. Amy hasn't been out with a boy yet, which is even worse than I am. I'm not exactly Miss Popularity like Audrey, but I've been on a couple of (rather awkward) dates. Either way, I'm not desperate enough to go to the mall with Jake Wylie, no matter what Eva and Melissa think.

"Sean has the N-Virus. He's already turned, according to the E-Network," Amy whispers.

I feel a little sick to my stomach, but part of me still doesn't believe it. "I'm sure that's a mistake."

"No. They're planning a telethon to raise awareness. It's gonna be on TV Saturday night. Everybody's going to be on it."

"Raise awareness?" That's stupid. People are dying of this virus, but it suddenly matters just because some silly celebrity has contracted it? I sigh. "If people aren't aware of the N-Virus by now, then they're idiots."

"Why are you mad?" Amy asks, furrowing her brow. "Sean McKinley is hot!"

"Was hot." I immediately wish I hadn't said that. It's cruel —not to Sean, but to Amy. "Sorry, Amy. It's just...they brought an N-Virus victim into the hospital yesterday, just after I started my shift. It was terrible."

"W-what happened? What did you do?"

I start to tell her about it, although I know better than to say too much. Dad doesn't like for me to tell people at school about what I see at the hospital any more than he wants me to tell Mom.

Suddenly, Mrs. Bell's there at the front of the classroom and I'm off the hook for the time being.

"Now, class. Take out last night's questions and pass them forward while I take attendance."

Amy leans closer to me. "What was it like?" she asks again.

"No talking, Amy," Mrs. Bell snaps.

"At lunch," I whisper. Lunch is three hours away. I only hope Amy might forget before then.

Of course, Amy doesn't forget as quickly as I hope and I try to avoid her as long as I can. I take my bag lunch (turkey, Swiss, and broccoli sprouts on rye on Wednesdays—Mom lives by schedules and healthy lunches) from my locker, scrape together enough change from the bottom of my book bag for a Diet Coke, and go out to eat alone on the football field bleachers.

At the far end of the field, a group of boys form a pickup game of soccer. Part of me wants to join in, but there aren't any other girls out there. I'll feel stupid. Besides, from here, I can watch Nick without anyone giving me the third degree.

Nick isn't half the soccer player I am, but he's good enough. And that's not being braggy, just truthful. Besides, boys with impossibly blue eyes, perfect skin, perfect teeth, and better hair than I have don't have to play like Messi to be interesting.

The sun beats down, warming the top of my head and my back through my thin blouse. The grass on the field below has just been mowed and the remaining morning dew glistens like little diamonds. I breathe in the sweet, green scent and for a moment a small, wondrous tingle of excitement oozes down my spine, just like when I was a little girl. Suddenly, I wish I could just skip the rest of school and just hang out in the sun, daydreaming.

Slowly chewing my sandwich, I create a silly imaginary scenario where Nick and I are all alone. Maybe Audrey has decided to see another guy or maybe she's joined the circus—I don't know or care. In that little five-minute mind-movie, my sister was simply gone.

I sip my Diet Coke, and then wad up the other half of my lunch and cram it back into the bag. Nick jogs by. Glancing my way, he waves, grinning. I wave back, relieved I'm far enough away that he can't see how I blush. I hope he never learns I've been watching him like some lovesick twelve-year-old.

Amy appears at the end of the bleachers, followed by Melissa and Eva. Brandi Allen, my one-time best friend, tags along a step behind. I try not to appear as disappointed as I feel.

"Cindy. What are you doing out here? You don't have anyone to talk to."

"I know."

"It's hot!" Melissa whines.

"I know," I agree again. Sure, they're my friends, but they're really slow to catch on sometimes.

"Amy said you promised to tell us about the N-Virus guy," Melissa presses.

"You never even mentioned it when I texted you last night," Brandi says. She draws her phone from her oversized purse and scrolls through the messages as if to prove her point. She and I have played on the same soccer teams since we were in first grade. She's good when she wants to be, but lately, she's more worried about meeting new guys than scoring goals. We were nearly like twins for years, but in the past year or so, we've drifted apart. I guess most people do eventually. I hate it...sort of.

It all started when I had my long hair cut shorter, just so we no longer looked like we were separated at birth. It's since grown back out, but looking back now, Brandi must have taken that move as a slap in the face. Oh well. We're all eventually going to go our own ways, anyway. High school is only a moment in the grand scheme of life. I remind myself of that almost every day.

Sometimes you aren't aware of how much another person holds you back until you're away from them. That was the way with me and Brandi. Brandi still wants me to wear my hair like hers, buy the same blouses and jeans. Even the same shoes.

Palmdale High is already filled with clones and I'm not about to jump in and be another one.

Plus, Brandi has become slightly pudgy since summer and I'm not about to chunk up just to be a bestie. She claims she was having issues at home, but the only issue anyone truly knows of is her addiction to white chocolate mochas from Starbucks.

"There's not so much to tell," I say. "A man came in the E.R. acting all weird." *Understatement of the year!* I start down the metal stairs.

"Like in a movie? Was he a zombie, do you think?" Brandi asks, excited.

"He was just some guy." I learned long ago it's easy to lie to people who aren't as intelligent as I am. Again, I'm not being braggy, only truthful. "He looked sick."

"Did he eat anyone?" Amy asks, making a face.

"He didn't eat anyone, Amy. That's stupid." But the image of Dr. Jacobs sitting on the E.R. floor with his arm gushing blood everywhere pops into my head.

"What about—"

The fire alarm blares, making us jump. I drop my lunch bag and bend down to get it. "There's nothing to tell," I say again, sounding more irritated than I meant to. I promised Dad I'd keep everything to myself and I keep my promises whenever I can. "Maybe there's something about it on the internet," I suggest, my tone easing a little.

Principal Warner's voice barks through the intercom sounding even more mechanical and shrill than usual.

"Students, report to your next classroom immediately. Anyone caught out of class at five past the hour will be written up."

"What's going on?" Amy whispers.

"How should we know?" Melissa snaps, rolling her eyes.

Before the virus, an announcement like that one could've only meant a few things—all of them bad.

The news is already making its rounds by the time we return to the west wing of the building. Audrey nudges my shoulder as she passes, heading to her fourth-period English class.

"Did you hear?" she asks. "There's a Shambler on campus."

"Are you kidding?" I'm unsure if I'm more surprised at the news or that Audrey is speaking to me in front of her super-cool, ultra-bitch posse.

"Maybe it's your boyfriend from yesterday," she smirks.

"I really doubt it," I answer, thinking about the hole suddenly appearing in the man's forehead—one heck of a magic trick. Audrey's already weaving her way down the hallway.

I shrug and shove through the dawdling hoard. The news of a Shambler on campus is a huge distraction, but I've already seen one up close and personal and isn't exactly keen to see another one so soon. Besides, Mr. Carlton's geometry class is next and word is his hair looks awesome today.

By soccer practice, the Shambler has been rounded up and things settle back into relative normalcy. As the coach calls it an afternoon, I notice Nick sketching under a tree on the far end of the field. I'm not sure what possesses me, but I decide to walk over as everyone else heads back into the locker room. I probably smell, but of course, at the moment I don't think of that. All I think of is his beautiful hair brushing the side of his neck and falling over one eye.

"Hi." I already feel stupid, but I'll appear even stupider if I take off now.

"Hey, Cindy," Nick says. He smiles and my knees suddenly feel like they might come unhinged.

"What are you drawing?"

"Just fooling around. Sit down."

I do, my naked knee grazing his. I shift away slightly. "I've always wanted to learn to draw," I say, which isn't altogether true. But gosh, does he smell good!

"You make it look so easy." I run my hand over my sweaty hair, hoping to calm down any errant strands. My ponytail has come loose and there's a mess of dirt caked on my shinguard.

"I should go. I'm a mess."

Nick glances at me and my face grows warm again, like it always does when he looks at me. "You should be. If you weren't messy, you didn't play hard enough. That's what my dad always said, anyway."

I laugh. "Well, then I played my ass off."

"You did," he agrees. "I watched." He turns his attention back to the page. The few lines that were there when I first walked up are magically developing into the lithe, muscular form of a superhero woman. "And no," he adds, "it isn't as easy as it looks. But I do it all the time. Practice makes perfect." He laughs slyly. "I'm beginning to sound like an old fart."

"But it's true," I say to him. He was watching me, is what I say inside my head.

"The key is to relax." Nick flips to a new page in the sketchbook and gives me the pencil.

"Here," he says. "Don't grip it like you're writing. Just let it rest between your finger and thumb."

He touches my fingers, placing them on the pencil. I love the way his hands feel, warm, a little rough.

"Now, try something easy," he tells me. "Like a circle. Keep your wrist loose and just make the shape."

I do, but the circle is more an egg than a wheel.

"Not bad," he says.

"Right."

"Not at all."

Although I could've stayed next to Nick the rest of the day, I gave him his pencil. "I guess I need to go before Coach locks up. Thanks."

"See ya, Cindy."

I jog back toward the locker room, smiling like a crazy girl and happy he can't see my face. Before I go inside, I turn to wave, but Nick is already gone.

CHAPTER 4

🌢

September 14
Cindy

The dreaded family meeting. I'm amazed that Audrey actually showed up. She skipped dinner, claiming to study at Nick's house. I have my doubts about that since Nick texted while she was out, looking for her. She can be such a bitch sometimes. Still, lucky her, in more ways than one—Mom decided to try her hand at Indian food. I don't know what it was, but I'm pretty sure it wasn't actually food.

I cover for her, of course, because I'm a bitch, too. And a selfish one, at that. If they break up, then Nick will move on (probably with someone much better for him than my own slutty sister), but I'm afraid I'll never see him.

The last time we had a family meeting was when Hurricane Irene appeared to be bearing down on Palmdale. Assuming the Audrey and I would be frightened, Mom and Dad explained why we were suddenly buying cases of bottled water and what would happen if we had to evacuate. Of course, that was four years ago and neither of us could drive. We were off the hook then. Not so much now.

I wasn't afraid then, but maybe I was too young to understand the gravity of the situation. I'm now four years wiser.

We converge in the family room and Mom switches off the television. The house falls strangely silent, and I don't much like it. It seems either music or the television is always on when we're all at home.

Audrey finally shows up, a half-hour late. She plops down on the sofa next to me, smelling like pot smoke and a healthy spray of the Blue Light perfume that I gave her last Christmas. Her hair's a mess, but Mom and Dad don't notice or else decide not to notice. I assume the latter. Boy, it must be nice to be Audrey...

She pulls out her cell phone and starts to text.

"Give it a break, Audrey," Dad snaps. "You can spare a few minutes, I think."

She breathes a hugely exaggerated sigh and slumps back into the sofa. Mom takes her phone and places it on the end table.

Then Mom squeezes between us, grinning like a girl. She had a couple of glasses of wine while making dinner and another afterward and is on her way to becoming buzzed. Mom's wine-induced silliness is a rarity, and usually a lot of fun, but tonight she holds it in check. The family meeting is serious business. Dad paces in front of us like a teacher in front of a class.

"Now, we all know what happened at the hospital yesterday, so don't need to go over the details of the N-Virus. Things are becoming more dangerous out there. I understand a carrier was spotted at school today," he says. "Did either of you see him?"

"I didn't," I answer.

"I did," Audrey says. "He was wearing a "Member's Only" jacket and a bad haircut."

"Really?" Mom asks.

"Well, I thought it was a Shambler. Turned out, it was just Mr. Winkler, the tenth-grade science teacher." Audrey giggles, sounding a little stoned.

Dad smiles tightly. "Okay, you've got one in. But this is really serious, girls." When he says "girls" like that, he always means Mom, too. I think it's sweet, but it makes Audrey cringe.

Maybe it's Dad's analytical mind that makes him want to plan ahead, but it's not like Shamblers are wandering down our street. I'm positive the government will come up with a solution before very long.

More than the analytical thinking, I imagine Dad has more than a touch of paranoia—from reading so many medical reports and things such as that. Either way, Dad's a planner, which is nice most of the time. Like vacations, travel soccer season, his week at work, or our college. It isn't as much fun when it's disease outbreaks for which he's planning.

I just hope this time it's a case of "better safe than sorry."

"Now, over the next few weeks, we're going to be stockpiling essentials. I've made a list of the items each of us will be in charge of gathering."

Audrey makes another stupid "I'm bored and dying" kind of sound and I want to slug her, but don't. Let her be the idiot. Maybe Mom and Dad will see it, finally. Dad passes a sheet of paper to each of us.

He's made four columns with each of our names at the top. Audrey begins reading the list following her name, unable to disguise the disgust in her voice.

"Toothpaste, toilet paper, tampons, soap, floss, shampoo. Bleach, white towels. Come on, Dad. Why do I need to be in charge of toilet paper? And tampons? Should I go and get a case at a time? That'll look cool." She rakes her fingers through her thick hair and pulls a face like just reading the list has exhausted her.

"Why does Audrey always get the fun ones?" I want to say, but again catch myself in time. It isn't a time to tease. I'll take the higher road.

"Cindy. For your items, Audrey will drive you. Pick up your items on the same day."

My list requires a visit to Home Depot. I need to get batteries—six-battery packages of each size, gasoline canisters for the emergency generator, and huge containers for saving water. I can't begin to picture what it'll be like if water runs out. Worse, I can't imagine what it might be like once the weather begins to grow colder and there's no electricity. I hate the cold and even in the South, it sometimes gets horribly cold.

Some of the other things I need to gather include utility knives, duct tape (the super tool), and a battery-powered radio.

"You girls help each other—Audrey, your list is Cindy's and vice versa. Go on Monday and Friday for the next four weeks and get as much as you can stuff into the X5."

Audrey quiets down when she learns she'll get to drive Mom's BMW SUV at least two days a week for a while.

"Your mother and I will be in charge of building the food supply, medication, and first aid items," Dad continues. His tone has lightened—he's planned a course of action. We'll all be okay if we simply follow it.

"Just think of this as a scavenger hunt," Mom says cheerfully.

Audrey shakes her head. "What's the prize? A giant box of Tampax?"

My mind drifts for a few moments. I try to imagine how they can be preparing for the coming apocalypse as the evening sun bleeds through the windows like gold paint and kids laugh and shout just outside on the street in front of our house.

Of course, this isn't the end of the world I tell myself. It's just September.

CHAPTER 5

●

September 15
Nick

Nobody can prepare for such an impact. Crashing metal. Glass sprays inward, into my face like a hundred bee stings. Headlights blinding, coming, coming, and the front of Dad's Volvo instantly rises in front of us, as crumpled as a piece of paper. Then it's over and the silence is worse than the crashing. My airbag deploys, throwing my scrawny thirteen-year-old body backward. Pain explodes from the middle of my chest outward. I can't catch my goddamned breath, I'm dying.

I black out, and there's peace.

Then I wake, gasping. How long has it been? Where am I? Smoke and steam cloud the air, stinking of gas and exhaust, but through it, I see Dad next to me, unmoving.

The driver's side airbag failed and he's taken the full impact of the collision. He's a big guy, my dad, but slumped over the steering column he's like some kind of stupid, broken doll. The steering wheel has bent nearly in half. I scream.

I scream.

I scream.

My earbuds are still screwed into my ears when I wake, Sun Airway's mechanical beats swirling in my brain. My t-shirt and shorts are glued to my skin with sweat—I'm burning up. I sit up and shake my head hard, trying to unclog the residue of the nightmare.

The same nightmare again. For the past four years. That isn't normal—Miles, my idiot stepdad, says so. I despise Miles, but I tend to agree with him on this. It isn't normal and no amount of spilling my guts to a therapist is going to help.

Still, I go through the motions because that keeps the peace. It keeps Mom happy, Miles quiet, and Micah, Miles's brat eight-year-old son, away from me.

The text came through at a little past nine p.m. but by then I'd fallen asleep

@ Tasha's. Practicing new cheers. <3 U!

I contemplate texting Audrey back, but instead set my phone aside and go back to my sketch pad. Screw her, anyway.

This sketch is a zombie from the *Dawn of the Dead* remake, with maybe a dash of *The Walking Dead* thrown in, drawn from memory. The only difference is this one is wearing a Palmdale High soccer uniform and has my hair and what is left of my face. Sure, it's one hell of a twisted self-portrait. I grin to myself and add a head on the ground in place of a soccer ball. I'll post it on my website tomorrow, once I finish shadows and other details. People buy these things, can you believe it? Zombie geeks are the most rabid buyers of my sketches, followed by the sci-fi nuts. Last month, I sold a simple Darth Vader ink and colored pencil for one hundred dollars. My savings account is getting nicely fat—I've made over fourteen hundred dollars since I started posting four months ago. Of course, I share this with nobody. Not even Audrey. I'm not that stupid.

When I finish, flip the sketchpad closed, and hide it in the middle of a stack of comic books, where it can't be found when Mom and Miles come in to snoop for the drugs they never find. I don't even like pot and booze is only an occasional vice, but that must be too hard to believe about a messed-up kid like me.

Miles would shit if he saw what I'm working on, but that's par for the course. Miles fills Mom's head with all kinds of bullshit. Dad's body wasn't cold in the grave before Miles and his rugrat started coming around, pretending they were "there to help." Miles is a cop and a stupid one at that. Dad said more than once that people who were bullies in high school became cops. That has to be Miles's deal. The bully has never left him. Miles has even tried to bully me into calling him "Dad." When I refused, Miles decided I wasn't worth his time. We live in the same house—Darryl Thatcher's house, by the way—but that's all. Miles and I've scarcely spoken to each other in three years. I want it that way.

I've learned to block out the pain that's permanently etched on Mom's face.

Fourteen hundred bucks isn't a lot, but it's a decent start. Once I get away from Palmdale, it'll be a cold day in hell before I come back, even for a visit. I've been accepted into the Academy of Art in San Francisco, but that's another secret. Sometimes I feel like living across the country will still be too close.

In California, nobody will know me. The pressure will be off. Audrey will forget me and I'll forget her. We'll finally have an excuse to part ways—that's all we're waiting for, anyway.

Besides, I'll miss Cindy more than Audrey. At least she acts like I'm more than just the other half of the most popular couple in school.

CHAPTER 6

●

September 16
Cindy

It's been two days since the Shambler came onto the campus. There are rumors of a county-wide curfew being issued, but nothing's happened so far. The sun hovers above the trees like a big orange ball and everything out front of our house has this soft red glow. Warmth. It's a good life, a normal life—a little boring, a little pale, I suppose. Later, maybe I'll understand how spoiled we've become by the ease of life in Palmdale. Never wanting for anything other than a few more minutes on the soccer field or an extra half-hour at the mall on a school night.

I wonder if the N-Virus will turn out to be the bitchslap of all bitchslaps. We live in a world of spoiled brats and it's reckoning time.

A typical Thursday night in the Scott household—Audrey leaving on a date with Nick and pretending she's still into him although we all know she's a cheat, and me, changing out of my practice gear. My legs still have the impressions of the shinguards—a nifty look if I want to go out in a skirt or shorts later. My knees are scraped—hardly the mark of sophistication, but what the hell. They're always scraped during soccer season. Besides, my big night out consists of the library or hanging with Amy or Melissa or someone other boring, only vaguely popular girl who can't scare up more than one or two dates a month. We might go to the J.V. game, which will mark us as eternally desperate for something to do, or we can go to the aforementioned mall, which also reeks of desperation—at least for me.

Maybe the N-Virus will get so out of hand, that we'll end up living inside the mall like in *Dawn of the Dead*.

September 21
Cindy

I didn't imagine things would change so much in only a week. My turn to volunteer at the hospital has come back around. Dad warned me things were spiraling downward at an alarming rate, but when I step through the automatic doors of the E.R., the scene is enough to make me want to turn around and flee back out into the sunny parking lot.

First, the stench hits me like someone shoved dirty socks in my face. The odor of illness permeates the air, like the stink of garbage left to putrefy out in the heat. I breathe through my mouth to keep from gagging. Throwing up is not a good impression on those who are already ill. Besides, Dad told me that the first time I let things in the E.R. get to me will be my last time volunteering.

Gurneys line both sides of the hallway, leaving only enough space to navigate through, each one occupied by a sweating, moaning body. The normally quiet corridor is terrible a choir of crying, grunting, and delirious babbling. Those who can pray softly—a troublesome murmur that makes the little hairs on my arms stand up.

I rush through, my head down. I don't want to look anyone in the face. I don't want to make eye contact with those I can't help.

I don't want to see anyone I might recognize.

I don't want to touch them or want them touching me, although I well know by now how the N-Virus is transmitted. Still, it's as if the simple act of dying is contagious and I want no part of it. Maybe Audrey's right. Is helping others so important that I'll risk my skin?

As I check in, I can't help noticing how everyone's demeanor has changed. The jovial, often caustic banter has morphed into this strange solemnness. Boisterous Sara only nods as I step behind the counter. I pull on a lab coat over the ill-fitting scrubs Dad has given me, a nameplate embossed with the legend "volunteer" pinned over my left breast. My name isn't Cindy now—it's "volunteer." I wonder if this is almost as desperate as going to a J.V. game or hanging out at the mall with a couple of semi-popular girls. A "volunteer"—I'm doing this for nothing in return.

Audrey's dumb attitude must have rubbed off on me today. I shove the notion aside and wait for someone to tell me what to do.

The bustle of the E.R. is beyond chaotic. There seems to be double the staff on the floor, everyone moving from gurney to gurney, checking blood pressure, listening to chests, adjusting blankets. It all amounts to very little, it seems.

I watch, uneasy, wondering where Dad is in all this... confusion.

"Make sure you wear a mask and gloves at all times today," someone says. I turn to find a tall, older nurse shoving a pair of latex gloves at me. "I'm Sylvia, by the way. I'm supposed to be retired, but it seems they need me. Don't you think?"

"Looks like it," I agree, tugging on the gloves. "Have you seen my dad? Dr. Scott?"

"You're Ben Scott's daughter? I should've guessed—you look like him. A good thing," she adds, winking. "What's your name?"

I told her.

Sylvia looks as though she's been on her feet for two days straight. Her mascara has smudged, making her appear as if she's been crying. "Your dad's around here somewhere."

I reach into the supply cabinet and take out a mask. It's only then that I realize my hands are shaking. Sometimes I get a case of nerves at the beginning of a soccer match—especially with a tough team—but this is something else. I'm suddenly terrified. For myself, for my dad, for my little town.

Sylvia notices. She touches my arm. "This will pass. All things do. We've had these halls filled with cases of flu and I thought we'd never get to everyone. Sometimes people die and that's the tough part of this job." She sighs. "But you're here because you want to help, right?"

"Yes," I answer, wondering if I'm just saying what I know people want to hear.

"Good, because we need you."

We need you. I almost want to look around and see who this woman is talking to. Either way, I put on the mask—it's one of those that covers my nose and mouth and has a clear plastic shield over my eyes. I feel like I'm playing dress-up.

That's until Sylvia leads me back down the packed corridor. She pulls me to her and relays commands into my ear. "We are here for comfort only, Cindy. At this point, all we can offer. These people are frightened. Because of the news, they know what they're in for. Don't get too close. Adjust their blankets, and talk to them a little. The incubation period can vary, depending on how much exposure these people have had. We have no way of knowing which of these people are in the last stages." She looks me hard in the eyes. "You understand what I mean by 'last stages,' don't you? That is when they become dangerous. That's when we need the guards to come in and handle things."

I nod and move to the first gurney closest to the entrance of the E.R. An elderly man lies there, staring straight up at the ceiling. Realizing I'm at his side, he turns his rheumy gaze to me.

"The mailman bit me. Can you believe it, dear? I thought he was handing me my mail and he just grabbed my hand and ...chomped down." He laughs shakily and holds up a bandaged hand between us.

He says something else, his mouth moving slowly, deliberately, but because of the constant moaning and crying, I can't hear him. I smooth his blanket, tell him the doctor would get him in soon, and pat his shoulder.

I move on to the next bed, taking a moment to look around at the scene that spreads before me. These are my people. That sounds silly, but it's true. My people. The ones I bump into at the supermarket or at the mall. Parents and grandparents of my friends. I don't know their names, but I know them. They are me and my family.

My stomach starts to ache. My heart starts to ache. The crying and writhing is so troubling, I wanted to just find Dad and leave.

Instead, I step over to the next bed, occupied by a woman who might be my mother's age. She doesn't notice me. Her eyes have grown as pale as dish water and her skin is the shade of the beige blanket that covers her. Her soccer mom's hair cut is flattened to her head, her sensible makeup is smudged around her eyes like bruises.

"The doctor will get to you in a few moments," I tell her, feeling like a liar. "Can I get you anything?"

No response. I don't touch her or pat her shoulder like I did the old man. Something tells me not to trust her. The stink of illness comes off of her in waves—perspiration, foul breath. I think she's soiled herself and is thankful she's covered with a blood-splotched blanket.

I'd start away from her when she suddenly sits up, her blanket falling away to expose the upper part of her body. What I see makes my stomach tighten and for a moment, I think I'll be sick. It's becoming apparent I'm not as immune to the horrors of the E.R. as I thought. The woman's entire left shoulder and the crest of her left breast have been chewed away. Dark, gnarled meat glistens like wet paint through her tattered blouse. Blood has soaked all the way through her blouse. I take a deep breath hoping to calm myself.

The pillow that was supporting her head has fallen to the floor and I stoop to get it. I want to get away from this patient. Sylvia made me understand none of these poor people have a chance, but this one is farther gone than the rest.

There's a feather-like caress on my shoulder and I jump and pull away. To hell with the pillow, the virus victims, and this hospital. But I'm going anywhere. The caress on my shoulder morphs into a vice grip on my hair. My head jerks back, the tendons in my neck scream, and I suddenly have an upside-down, close-up view of the chewed-up woman. Her white lips pull back into a wolf's snarl, bearing her nicotine-stained teeth. She rips away my mask, her putrid breath wafting into my face making my throat close up for a moment.

I can't speak. I can't move. Her pale eyes have me hypnotized, nearly. But the young woman who's sitting on the gurney across the narrow hallway from us does scream. She springs up and latches her hands around my attacker's throat and begins to shake her hard, which isn't a lot of fun, as my attacker still has hold of my hair. I'm being thrown from side to side by my hair, my scalp screaming.

Finally, I find my voice and scream for my Dad, Sylvia, for whoever can hear. Dad materializes at my side like my guardian angel, seemingly sensing that I'm in danger. I can't tell what he's doing, but in an instant, the hold on my hair relents and I fall on my ass to the floor. A shrill scream rings out and is quickly muffled. I jump to my feet and turn around. Dad pulls the woman's blanket over her face, then twisted it into a knot at the back of her head. The fabric is drawn tight over her, but I can still make out the hollow of her open mouth, the bump of her squashed nose, and the shallower indentions of her eyes.

Just then, a guard I don't recognize bursts through the doors at the end of the hallway, his belly swaying as he runs, his gun already drawn.

He trains it on the young woman who has helped me.

"Wait! She's safe," I cry, jumping in front of her and pointing at the screaming woman.

Dad drags the woman to the floor, the blanket still wrapped around her head. He rolls her onto her belly and places a knee on the middle of her back. She's still trying to fight, but Dad's too heavy for her to do any more damage.

"Help me, will you?" Dad snaps at the guard.

For a moment, the guard only stands there, staring stupidly, until Sylvia nudges his shoulder.

"We can't let her get away. She's contagious," she tells him.

I help the young woman, my savior, back onto her gurney.

"Thank you," I say as I pull her blanket back up. My hands are still shaking, and my heart still thumping in my chest like a flat tire.

The young woman doesn't have any visible bite wounds, so I wonder how she contracted the N-Virus. Her pallor is still good, but her eyes are beginning to grow pale and dull. I'm learning very quickly that the whitish irises are the most telling symptom of the early stages of the virus. I feel so bad for her—she could've been me or Audrey.

"Can't I get you anything?"

She smiles. "A cure, maybe?"

"I wish I could," I tell her. "More than anything, I wish I could."

She senses I'm looking for a bite mark. She holds up her arm and removes a small bandage that's taped to the underside of her bicep, partially hidden by the sleeve of her black t-shirt.

"It's right here," she says, pulling back the bandage and showing me the small wound. It's a ragged little hole, maybe as big around as a silver dollar. "A kid did it. A fucking little girl." She laughs bitterly. "I don't know where came from or where she went. She chomped down on me in the parking lot of the Starbucks. All I wanted was a mocha Frappuccino before I started my shift at the restaurant. I work at Applebee's on seventeen."

I nod, suddenly wanting to cry. This girl goes out for a coffee before work and now this. She's going to die. Worse, she knows she's going to die. I swallow hard and give her a quick, timid hug before Dad notices. "Thanks for saving me."

She sinks back onto the gurney and turns her head. "It was nothing. I have nothing to lose, now, anyway."

Dad comes over and wraps his arm around my shoulders. He leads me away before I can let the woman see me crying, out into the bright daylight. The sun hurts my eyes and his fingers burrow into the flesh of my upper arm painfully.

Outside is strangely silent compared to the noisy commotion of the E.R. Finally, Dad lets go of me and I rub where gripped my arm. I'll discover bruises there when I shower later. At first, I think he's angry with me, but when I get a good look at his face, I know otherwise.

"Are you bitten?" he asks, his voice cracking. "Did she scratch you?" He takes my face in his big hands and stares into my eyes. He's crying, his face streaked and shiny with tears. My dad. Crying.

"N-no. That girl stopped her. I'm okay."

He tilts my head this way and that, examining my throat, then lifts my hair and checks the back of my neck.

"I don't see any blood. You're sure?"

I nod. I laugh a little, unable to stop myself. Dad's always as cool as a cucumber, as they say. His reaction is worrying, to say the least. I'm not sure I understood the gravity of what's happening around us until now.

"I'm fine. Really, Dad."

"Okay." He puts his arms around me and clutches me to him like he'll never let me go again. I feel completely safe.

Later I'll remember this was one of the last times I felt that way. For an instant, I'm six years old again, having woke with nightmares. Dad always made the monsters go away.

"You're finished volunteering until we get this virus under control," he says.

The sense of relief that washes over me is overwhelming and surprising. I've never quit anything—it's one of my quirks, I suppose--and I've been determined not to quit volunteering, either. But how I want to be away from this hospital. I want to stop pretending I'm afraid of the dying and the undead. Dad is my out and I love him for it.

"Dad, I can't breathe," I say after a moment, my words muffled against his chest.

"Sorry." He lets me go, but not before planting a kiss on top of my head, just like he used to when I was small. I'll never volunteer again. However, this isn't the end of my visits to Palmdale Memorial.

CHAPTER 7

October 3
Cindy

School's a mess. For most people, especially people like me, who have gone to the same schools in the same community, with the same people their entire lives, school can become the only constant, the only comfort. It can be the only connection to a normal world when the world around them goes to hell.

I remember once, when I was in the eighth grade, a terrible thunderstorm came up over the school. For a while, it felt as though we were at school at night. There were warnings of tornadoes in the area and the teachers grew as nervous as cats with the shits.

Either way, school has been my constant, until now. Now, every day is like that dark day in the eighth grade. The school is on continuous lockdown, from the morning bell until dismissal. Armed police officers escort us to and from our cars or the buses. We're no longer allowed outside for lunch or even gym class. The track team is running laps in the gymnasium. Some of the dads stand guard around the fields during baseball and soccer practice, pacing back and forth like soldiers in golf shirts and boat shoes, armed with expensive hunting rifles and shotguns.

Dad says something terrible will eventually come of that arrangement. Someone is going to be shot and it isn't going to be a Shambler. It'll be over football or maybe it will be an accident. Either way, tragedy is so close—from the virus or from our own doing.

Attendance is noticeably down. The hallways are empty. People I used to see every day seem to have vanished. I wonder if they've contracted the virus. Did they turn? Most of my best friends are still coming, however, and as annoying as they are, I'm thankful they're okay.

Still, the notion of girls just like myself wandering around, dead, but not quite dead, hungry for flesh... It's a horrible thing to think of.

The evening unfolds like most other evenings. It's one of those nights that ends up a "family" night. I sit on the sofa, reading my iPad one moment and watching the tube the next. Audrey keeps her phone in her fist, texting constantly. There's something stupid on television about the N-Virus. Mom drinks her glass (or glasses) of wine and Dad pretends he isn't worried.

The atmosphere is heavy with tension and there's this unspoken urge to be together. We'll probably be over it by breakfast, but now it's there and it's real. If we're all together, we'll be okay. We're safe. Nothing, not even a virus, can touch us.

Everyone turns in early. I climb into bed, exhausted, despite the light soccer practice. I feel as if a stone has been placed on my back and the only relief is getting into my bed and pretending everything is normal for a few moments before I drift into sleep.

It's soothing to hear my parents through the walls of my bedroom while I wait for sleep to come. After what is unfolding, just knowing they are only feet away is comfort. Just like when I was very small and I fell asleep to the low sound of their voices. Whispers, a laugh. Sure, it's voyeuristic and probably weird, at my age, but I'm not sure I care now how weird it is.

A person comes to learn what things spell comfort for them—the smell of their grandmother's house, the sound of rain against the window, sunshine painting a soccer field in light and warmth. Christmas. The voices of your family.

Silence isn't precious. It's smothering and troubling.

But back to my parents. As I said, I'm not a perv, but sometimes I want to know what they're saying. Both Dad and Mom have a thing where they still want to protect me and

Audrey from the truth. Still, it's easy to regret listening sometimes.

"Everything is moving quickly. The virus is spreading here at a faster rate than we anticipated it would," Dad says, and follows it with a tired sigh. "The hospital has become overwhelmed. And it's only going to get worse."

"How long do we continue to pretend life is normal?" Mom asks.

"As long as we can remain safe while doing it, I suppose."

I hear the clink of Mom's bracelets as she undresses for bed. "I doubt that will be very much longer." A pause. The creak of the bed. "Still. It's awful, don't you agree? Especially what Johnson's is planning to do with that cemetery," she says.

"The Pastures is nothing out of the ordinary. It's already happening in other areas. Besides, what would we do, if it were one of us? They're still walking around. Are they alive? I don't believe so. But they are not dead as we understand death. The patients I've seen were clinically dead, but..." Dad adds something else, but it's too muffled to hear, and then, "...like another state altogether. Do you want to be the one to 'pull the plug,' so to speak?"

"Maybe they'll find a cure and bring them back," Mom says, briefly hopeful.

I strain, listening, hoping for the response I want to hear. Instead, I'm rewarded with silence. It hangs for a long moment, like a weight suspended in the air.

"But what if there's not? Do we just allow them to wander around, mad with rage and hunger until they rot away?" Dad's voice grows more forceful. This is something I'm not used to hearing. The only person around our home who raises her voice is Audrey. I can almost see his face, his brows together, his mouth in a tight line. "You have to understand something, Meg. This isn't a fucking cold."

I decide not to hear anymore. I'm sick to my stomach. I really should move my bed to the opposite wall, but then I'll hear Audrey on the phone or Skype with her bitchy girlfriends or sweet-talking Nick because that's what she does to get her way. Worse, I'll hear her with Tommy Barker and that makes me sicker than anything else. Maybe I'm just stupid, but how is it so easy for some people to lie? Sure, everyone tells small, harmless lies. But lies like the ones Audrey tells Nick really hurt.

Typically, the nights in Palmdale are insanely quiet. I've had people who've moved here from other cities comment that the silence is disconcerting and something they have to grow used to. But the past couple of nights have been different. Somewhere close by, a police siren wails. A dog starts up, trying to compete. Before long, it sounds like a dozen dogs chiming in, each one trying to outdo the other.

Tired of the noises and the talk, I grab my iPad, wedge the earbuds into my ears, and listen to an older Muse album I've stored in my cloud. I scroll through the newest books I've downloaded. I've purchased every "realistic" zombie novel I could find if there's any such thing. Jonathan Mayberry, Courtney Summers, Amanda Hocking. I even have Brooks' Zombie Survival Guide. I'm not sure what I stand to gain from these books—these people didn't write stories anticipating an actual zombie apocalypse—but maybe I can get an idea. I tried video downloads a few nights ago, but it was a brief experiment. *The Night of the Living Dead* is slow and cheesy and not especially interesting. Others, like the newer *Dawn of the Dead* and *The Walking Dead*, are just so much like the real thing (I can't believe I'm writing this), that I can't watch, even though I know it's a lot of makeup and syrupy blood. All I can think of is how horrible it would be to become one of those "things."

I close my eyes and let the music fill my head and my mind. Soon, I drift off into a light sleep. I dream.

Nick's outside, wandering around the front yard.

I tap on the window, excited to see him. He looks up at me.

He's changed.

I wake, the earbuds tangled in my hair. My face is feverish and wet with slick tears.

CHAPTER 8

October 11
Cindy

I usually try to sleep late on Saturdays when we don't have a soccer game, but this morning I wake as soon as the sunshine touches my window. I lie still for a moment, a rail of sunshine warming my face and my arm. The house is still quiet. Mom and Dad are still in bed. For a few moments, I listen to the nothingness that fills the house and pretends things are perfectly normal. Outside, I think I can hear little kids playing.

Audrey trudges in, just out of bed. It's something she never does and in that moment, when the sun's too orange through the window and the shadows too heavy to make things pretty, she looks beautiful, anyway. For this instant, I'm in awe of my sister.

Well, her physical beauty, anyway. A bitch is a bitch, no matter how perfect the wrappings are.

She pushes the heavy veil of her hair back from her face and moves toward the window.

"How can you sleep?"

I shift under the covers, realizing I'm sweating. I was much too warm.

"I don't know. I guess I was more tired than I thought."

"I guess," Audrey says. She hugs herself, staring outside. "There's a strange woman out there, you know. I've been watching her for an hour now."

I throw my covers aside and climb from bed. My skin prickles into gooseflesh at the sudden chill of the air making me want to shrug back into the warmth of my bed. I join my sister in front of the window, the sheer curtain like some sort of dumb shield although the woman isn't looking our way. Audrey's warm shoulder brushes mine. For the first time, I notice I'm taller than she is. She was always my big sister, but suddenly I'm the taller one.

"Where?" I ask, rubbing the sleep from my eyes. All I can see is Mr. Graves putting up Halloween decorations way too early. A few styrofoam gravestones pepper his lawn and a gauzy ghost hangs from his oak tree, dancing lazily in the breeze.

"There. Just below the basketball hoop."

"Do you think she's a Dead Head?"

"Probably."

"Do you recognize her?" I ask.

"Can't tell from here."

The woman starts down our driveway, then stops at the mailbox, swaying for a moment like she might fall.

"I've seen Mrs. Akers do that at our barbecues," Audrey comments lightly.

It's true. If anyone loved a margarita, it's Mrs. Akers. We laugh. At this moment, I truly love my sister. We're a pair, part of a team. If we gain anything from this N-Virus mess, maybe it'll be closeness. I've only felt that way a handful of times in my life.

The woman reached out, her gnarled hand shaking, and pulled open the door of the mailbox.

Audrey pulls back the curtain, pulls open the window, and leans out to get a better look. "I didn't think they could do much, except bite and moan."

"Dad thinks they retain some memory. Not much, but a trace of little everyday things—getting the mail, maybe showing up places they loved."

"I guess I'd find a way over to the mall," Audrey says.

"I'd end up on the soccer field at school," I tell her.

"God, you're a nerd," she whispers. We laugh again, but this time it's forced, uncomfortable.

"Should I tell Dad?" I ask.

"Don't bother. Someone will discover her soon enough." I glance at her. She actually looks a little sad. It surprises me. Maybe she does have a heart somewhere behind her "Class-A Tits," (her words, not mine).

"Audrey? Are you afraid?"

"No. I mean Dad and Mom'll take care of us. As long as we're careful, we'll all get through this."

"I love you, Audrey," I say, and immediately feel silly.

"Love ya, too. Now don't be such a baby." She shoves my shoulder playfully and leaves my room.

Remember those panic-inducing articles on Yahoo about the avian flu? We're still going to school. My parents still work and go out for cocktails on Thursdays. There'll be a football game on Friday night. A soccer match on Saturday morning. People still act like Halloween monsters aren't real although we're seeing them on the news in a constant loop. Everyone still plans for dances and dates, vacations, and holidays. I saw a Christmas ad for Disney World last week, but Halloween hasn't even gotten here yet.

All those things are the same, but there's a difference. Not the obvious changes like armed guards, and the newly implemented curfew, but something that's intangible. It's a sense of desperation, a feeling of time growing short.

It's like the world is ending, but maybe if everyone just continues with life, ignoring it, it won't happen. The N-Virus is like a gigantic asteroid hurdling toward Earth. Maybe it'll just miss us. It's not like in the movies—it's a slow unfolding and everyone's hands are tied.

October 19
Cindy

Dad just caught a Shambler going through the trashcans. Garbage pick-up has become irregular and now the trash piles up until Dad drives it over to the recycling center a couple of times a week. He complains about how it smells, even bagged up. He says it smells like them, the Shamblers.

I'd just climbed into bed when I heard a crash outside, just below my bedroom window.

"Dad?" I call down the hall. "Did you hear that?"

"Yeah." Mom and Dad pad into my bedroom. They'd already gotten into bed, both of them in their pajamas. Mom looks just like Audrey with her face scrubbed free of makeup. Makeup makes the lines under her eyes more pronounced, but I'd never tell her that. The wrath of Mom, and all that.

Dad takes off his reading glasses and sticks them on the top of his head. "I'll check it out. Maybe it's just a dog. Or a raccoon." He doesn't sound sure about either one. He and Mom disappear down the hall.

Audrey comes in, raking the brush through her hair in a way that always looks positively painful. She's dressed in a pair of boy shorts and one of Dad's oversized t-shirts that she manages to make look good.

"What's going on?" she asks.

"Heard something," I tell her. "I wonder if it's a Shambler."

"Maybe. I keep hearing about sightings," Audrey says. "It's weird. The news is saying these people are dead. Dead on their feet." She laughs.

"Did you go out with Nick?" I ask. Sure it isn't any of my business, but I still have to know.

"Nope. Besides, what's the point? We have to be home like we're in the third grade because of that stupid curfew." She switches the brush to her other hand and starts abusing the other side of her head. She doesn't bother elaborating and really doesn't have to. I know.

"Why would you do that to him?" I want to shove her out the window. So much for that sisterly closeness that I felt a couple of days ago.

She stops brushing. "Because I can," she adds, narrowing her eyes, "and why does it matter to you, anyway?"

"Because he's a good guy. He doesn't deserve that." I put my iPad aside and push past her. I can't stand to be in the same room with her any longer.

Downstairs, I find Mom in a near-panic, just inside the French doors that open to the back deck. "There's one of those ... things out there." She has her robe gathered tightly at her neck and I want to tell her it's only a Shambler, not a vampire.

I peer around her and out into the night. Maybe Audrey's right—maybe the infected are actually dead. It's cool outside with the first breaths of autumn and steam rises from Dad's face like funny speech balloons in a comic book. But around the Shambler's face is nothing. There's no indication he's breathing at all.

This Shambler must have been one of the first infected. He's rotten, part of his cheeks thin enough to expose white glints of bone in the porch light. He isn't wearing shoes or socks and his feet are filthy—I'm not sure why I feel like I need to look at this man's feet. He's quite tall but bent like an overworked accountant. Maybe death has beaten him down. A rather expensive-looking tie hangs crooked from his scrawny neck. His white button-down shirt is untucked in the front. Filthy as are his pants and feet.

He snarls at Dad and Dad raises his three wood, but the Shambler only turns his attention back to the garbage can. Dad glances back at us and shrugs. "Call the police," he tells Mom.

Mom rushes past to get her phone and I stay by the door, my heart pounding, afraid the infected man might suddenly lunge at him just as that man had lunged at me at the hospital. The Shambler only removes a Styrofoam meat tray, still coated with dark, running blood from last night's hamburgers. He brings it to his rancid face, appears to smell it, and then begins licking it rabidly.

I want to turn away, but can only watch. Like a train wreck, as they say. You can't look away, no matter how much you want to.

"Gross, Dad!" Audrey cries like Dad's fault. I haven't noticed she's crept up. "Kill it!"

"He's not it, Audrey," Mom says. She pushes past us and opens the door a few inches. The cool air and the stink of the Shambler waft in and I block my nose with the back of my hand and breathe through my mouth.

"The police are on the way, Ben," Mom says. "Now get inside."

"In a minute," Dad says, but he moves closer toward the door. The Shambler continues cleaning the meat tray with his rotting tongue, oblivious to any of us.

"Mom," Audrey gripes. "Look at him. He's putrid. Disgusting. He's dead, Mom."

"Audrey, please!" Mom snaps.

Audrey sighs, tosses her hair, and goes back upstairs.

A thin red light suddenly floods the side yard and bleeds onto the back patio.

Mom lets out a long, relieved breath. "They're here."

A pair of officers round the side of the house; decked out in riot gear, face smeary behind Plexiglas face guards, chests thick inside the protective vests. Both have their revolvers drawn.

"Back away from the intruder, Dr. Scott. We'll handle this now," comes a muffled voice that I instantly recognize as Andrew Blackmon, who, at twenty-eight, still lives with his mother on the other side of the neighborhood. I can't determine who the other officer is behind his mask.

I'm not sure if the Shambler senses something, but he jerks around, dropping the meat tray. Moaning loudly, he steps toward Andrew, his arms outstretched ahead of him, his gnarled fingers pulling into bony claws. He reminds me of a monster in a cheesy old horror movie, but this is no movie. It's all too real and in the moment, it's all over.

Without hesitation, the other officer fires, taking off the top of the Shambler's head in a rain of dark, chunky brain matter, blood, and skull fragments.

Mom screams and Audrey immediately reappears in the kitchen. "What the hell was that?" she cries. "Is Dad okay?" She races to the window to check for herself.

I'll go out the next morning, just after Dad has sprayed away the mess with the hose, and see pocks in the wood siding where pieces of bone have embedded. Thankfully, a transport shows up for the body before I wake for school.

No matter what happens up until that moment is nothing compared to the surreal fear of what comes next. Officer Andrew then turns to my dad, his gun still drawn, but now points right at Dad's chest. Dad drops the golf club and raises his hands.

"What's he doing, Mom?" Audrey says, her voice little more than a desperate whisper. "What's he doing?"

Neither Mom nor I can answer. We only watch helplessly.

"We're you bitten, Dr. Scott?"

"No. He never touched me," Dad answers. He sounds completely calm.

"Maybe we should take him in," the other officer barks from behind his mask.

"Here," Dad says, stretching his arms out in front of him. "Check, if you want. He never touched me." He pushes the loose sleeves all the way back to expose his unmarred arms.

Officer Andrew puts away his gun and steps forward. Quickly, he examines the front and back of Dad's arms and nods. "He's good," he tells his partner.

"This is our second nuisance call tonight, Dr. Scott."

"Nuisance call," Audrey mutters. "That's what they're calling it?"

Eventually, the cops leave and the four of us sit at the kitchen table for a while, allowing our hearts to slow and our frayed nerves to relax as much as they can. Mom microwaves for mugs of hot cocoa and we drink, not speaking very much.

My eyes drift toward the back door, morbidly searching for another stray.

Nothing else happens that night, but when I climb into bed, I lay quietly, listening for the comforting voices of Mom and Dad to drift through the wall of my bedroom. Instead comes the low murmur of a cable news station. I shove my earbuds deep into my ears to block the sound but don't bother turning on any music. Eventually, I fall into a thin, troubled sleep. I don't remember any dreams when I wake up the next morning.

October 24
Cindy

Let me tell you about Sunday nights. Sunday nights in the Scott house have become what's commonly known (between me, Dad, and Audrey) as "really bad food night." This is the one night of the week when all of us are home together for dinner, so it's Mom's opportunity to show off her cooking skills. Unfortunately, Mom's cooking skills are frighteningly limited because Grandma never took the time to show her how to cook. Grandma never cooked, even when Grandpa was alive. They ate out almost every night—Italian on

Monday, Chinese on Tuesday, seafood on Wednesday, and so on. So, Mom is determined Audrey and I will learn to cook. Even if it kills us all (bad choice of words, maybe).

To make matters worse, Mom loves trying new and "exotic" recipes, something that makes Audrey complain even more than usual. "Why don't we master one of the regular dishes before trying these weird ones?" she always suggests.

In the "Gospel According to Audrey," "regular dishes" are things like mac and cheese or vegetable lasagna. "Weird" recipes consist of anything not on the menu at P.F. Chang's or The Cheesecake Factory.

Mom removes a wooden cutting board from a lower cabinet and then slips a big, scary-looking knife from a butcher block. She inexpertly skins a large white onion and slices it into thin slivers. "You girls need to know how to cook. One day you'll be out on your own and you can't eat out every night."

"Of course, we can," Audrey says.

Dad sits on a high stool at the counter, pretending to read the news from his iPad, but really watching his girls at work.

"You'll never catch a man, if'n you cain't cook," he says, pulling an exaggerated Southern drawl. He sips a beer and Mom moves over to sneak a drink every now and again. It's odd, watching Mom drink from a squat brown bottle. She usually prefers wine—a lady's drink, she's said more than once—but tonight is light and playful, despite the deadhead sightings and the added security at this weekend's soccer match.

For this evening, we're four people, safe in our home as the rain pelts the windows and the roof and squalls blow in off the ocean. The N-Virus, the death, and the uncertainty are forgotten for a while.

"I like learning how to cook," I say, meaning it. I do enjoy the notion of sitting down to a dinner that I've made. Provided it's edible. What we're trying to make this night is Tandoori Chicken. Mom even went to Crate and Barrel for a clay cooker, which is a much prettier pot than the regular old stainless, copper-bottoms we normally use.

I glance down at the recipe sheet Mom printed from the internet, then take the plain yogurt from the refrigerator.

"You'd say that," Audrey snaps, nudging me aside with her elbow. She takes the yogurt from me and pops the lid. Dipping her finger in, she tastes the smooth cream and pulls a disgusted face. "Yuck! I hope the end result is better than this!"

"We could just have collard greens and pork chops," Dad offers, knowing how Audrey detests "hillbilly food," as she calls it. I giggle and rummage the spice rack for cardamom and ground cloves, doubting we have either.

Things go pretty much great until the clay pot becomes too hot. As the pungent smoke overtakes the kitchen, Dad flips on the exhaust fan and grabs a pair of pot holders. He moves the pot to the sink while Mom fans the smoke around with a dish towel. Audrey bitches about the smell wrecking her hair while I open the windows in the kitchen and the dining room, but only a few inches. I don't want to take a chance on an unwanted visitor.

Dad removes the lid and we all peer down at the charred remains of our special chicken dinner. "I guess the chicken's off the menu," he announces, not sounding very disappointed.

We end up having Hamburger Helper and a bag of frozen Shoepeg corn.

One of the last somewhat normal nights we'll ever have will always be marked by the memories of burned chicken and laughing over a dinner of salty pasta and cheese.

CHAPTER 9

🝆

November 6
Cindy

Audrey and I seldom do anything together. Most of the time, I'm happy enough to pass her in the hallway at school or at home without a word. Some sisters just aren't close and that's just the way it is until Mom and Dad started "forcing us" on these weekly excursions for supplies. Today is Home Depot, which looks like a real chore at first. That is until Audrey announces she's going to pick up Nick on the way.

"Don't tell Mom and Dad," she says, easing the BMW to a stop in front of Nick's big, ultra-modern house. His mother and late father had money—maybe even more than our parents—but he makes no show of it. Still, I'm pretty sure that was the main reason Audrey chose him in the first place.

The SUV's reflection is super-long and narrow like a funhouse mirror in the all-glass facade that surrounds the front entrance. The shrubs and decorative grasses have gone wild as a jungle—lawn maintenance is no longer on anyone's priority list. As we wait, I wonder what would happen if the Shamblers came in numbers like they did in those movies.

I shiver at the thought but push it away as soon as Nick emerges, jogging toward us.

"Climb into the backseat, numbskull," Audrey tells me, not too unkindly, and then adds "and try not to drool."

My face gets hot and I shift to the middle and then slide between the seats into the back. Nick hops in, gives Audrey a perfunctory kiss, and closes the door.

"Hey, Cindy," he says.

"Hi," I mumble. Boy, he smells so nice. Unlike most of the immature jerks at school, Nick knows how to properly wear cologne. He doesn't drown himself in it, he puts just enough on for anyone who's lucky enough to be close to him to notice.

"So? What's up?" he asks, buckling up. "Where're we heading?"

"Should we surprise him?" Audrey asks, grinning wickedly. She glances at me in the rearview mirror as we pull away.

"If we tell him, he might hop out and run away," I answer.

"Come on!" Nick cries. "I skipped out on going to my Granny's for this."

"Well, prepare yourself," Audrey says. "We're going to Home Depot."

"You're kidding."

Neither of us answers.

"Aren't you?"

"No. That's where we're going. Dad wants us to get supplies," I confess.

"For the zombie apocalypse," Audrey adds.

"Fun." Nick slumps against the seat. "You know what that place is gonna be like? It's been like the day before a hurricane for weeks. I went over there with Miles last weekend. People were getting ugly over plywood and tomato seeds."

"Tomato seeds?" Audrey asks.

"Don't ask me why," Nick tells her with a shrug.

I say nothing. I know why. It's like a cloud at the horizon on a sunny day at the beach. It's okay at the moment, but a storm's coming. You can either prepare early and pack your things ahead of time or you can throw everything together once you see the first strike of lightning and run like hell.

Nick wasn't exaggerating. Home Depot is a madhouse. Droves of men in sweaty t-shirts that don't quite fit over their swinging tummies push carts and dollies through the store, piled with plywood, buckets, bleach, and duct tape. Some have generators and others have propane tanks. At the front, there are only two lines, both snaking down the nearest aisles, thirty or more deep.

"You've gotta be screwing me," Audrey whispers as we go inside.

"No wonder your dad sent you two," Nick says. "He's a smart guy."

I look around and spot a shopping cart abandoned near the front doors. I grab it just as an older man reaches for it.

"Here, you go ahead," I say, letting go of the handle. He takes it and hustles away without a word or a glance my way.

"Nice manners," Nick calls after him, and lower, he adds, "asshole."

"Let's try to grab some of the small things that we can just carry," I suggest, taking the list Dad gave me from the pocket of my jeans. We've been making these trips for weeks, missing out on this item or that. Deliveries are still being made to the stores, but they are increasingly irregular.

It quickly becomes clear that luck isn't on our side today, either. Duct tape is gone, as are most other kinds of tape. The only batteries left are those rectangular nine-volts that don't fit anything but the smoke detectors. Water canisters, gas canisters, and most other containers that will hold water are gone, leaving the shelves strangely empty.

Nick does grab up the last five starter fire logs, although they aren't on my list. "It's getting colder. I know how girls are—always cold."

"Hardly," Audrey counters. "I'm hot."

Nick flashes one of his patented cute-boy smiles. Glancing at me, he shrugs. "I guess I was wrong."

"I think it's a good idea," I tell him. He's right—at least about me. I've never been one for cold weather. I mutter a "thank you," wanting to kiss him instead.

Near the garden department checkouts, things are getting ugly between a couple of men who are on the wrong side of middle age. "You stole that goddamn lantern off my cart. It was one like that and you just took it," a sloped-shouldered guy in an Izod golf shirt and an expensive haircut shouts. His wife, timid and sweet-faced, touch him.

"It doesn't matter, Hal," she says, barely loud enough to be heard. "We have several at home."

"Better listen to your wife, old man," barks a man who looks to be even older than the first guy. He storms forward, two boxes containing halogen lamps tucked awkwardly under one arm. His thin lips pull back, revealing crooked and yellowing teeth as he shoves the other old man. The sweet-faced wife screams, her hand flying to her chest as her hubby stumbles backward and plops on his ass.

Part of me wants to scream at them, to scream at the people standing around watching, not helping, but who am I? I'm not helping, either. I'm getting what I can use just like everyone else.

Nick nudges Audrey with his elbow. "Let's get out of here," he says. He weaves through the gathering throng of rubberneckers, holding Audrey's hand, and I jog to keep up. With the scuffle, nobody seems to pay attention and we move to the front of one line. Audrey pays with Dad's credit card and leaves with only the handful of useless batteries and the logs. Home Depot has been a bust, but instead of going home, Audrey hangs a left onto Highway 17 and heads north. Apparently, in her world, there's no bad time to go to the mall. Even as society crumbles around her.

The parking lot looks like it probably does on Christmas Day. Of course, I've never been out on Christmas to know for sure, but it's empty save for a few cars and pickups parked near the entrance to the food court and the middle doorways. Trash—fast food wrappers, newspapers—blow leisurely around the pavement. It's strange, to see trash everywhere like this. Normally, Palmdale Mall is fairly pristine.

Audrey nearly pulls onto the curb in front of Bed Bath & Beyond and for a moment, I want going to credit her with some good thinking. I never considered a bath and kitchen store, but why not? There might be something useful in there.

Of course, I should know better.

"I'm not taking any chances," Audrey says, climbing out. "With nobody around, this is prime territory for Shamblers, I'll bet. Besides, this entrance is closer to American Eagle."

"Dad didn't say we could do that," I argue, jogging to catch up with my sister's long, purposeful strides. Nick lingers behind. When I glance back at him, he's cautiously scanning the parking lot.

"This is the way I see it, baby sis. We're taking valuable time to pick up this shit we're probably not even going to need. We deserve something new, don't you think?"

"I think you're living in another reality," I say. "Look around you. It's Friday afternoon and there's hardly anyone here." I'm sick of her selfishness and her stupidity. "Let me have the card."

"No." Audrey raises her chin in that dumb haughty way she has. I step forward, my fist clenched. I want to hit her suddenly. I want to knock that bitchy look off her face; I want to floor her.

Nick must sense it. He steps between us, his arms out, a small grin touching the corners of his mouth. "Let's not fight, ladies. Audrey, let's check out the sporting goods store and maybe Sears first. Then we can check out A&E and Hollister."

He waits for a response, but Audrey cocks one hip out and sulks.

"Okay?" Nick slips his hand along my sister's neck and pulls her closer. He kisses her and I look away. Audrey doesn't deserve any of us—especially a guy like Nick.

"All right," she agrees, rolling her eyes. "But make it quick. I hate sports stores."

Our footsteps echo in the stillness of the mall and my mind fills with scenes from the Dawn of the Dead remake. What if we discover the exits are clogged with Shamblers and we can't get back to the Beemer? What will we do? The idea of living inside a shopping mall with Nick isn't completely unappealing, but I'm positive I need to get away from Audrey as soon as possible. Or else, I'm going to snatch her bald.

The crowd (if you could call it that) at Dick's Sporting Goods isn't anywhere as thick and unruly as the one at Home Depot. It's probably because everything that appears to be of some use is gone. The shelves in the camping and hunting department are picked bare. However, if you need baseball equipment, you're in business.

Nick grabs a big barreled aluminum bat and takes a few fairly inexperienced swings. Nick's a soccer player, like me. "You know, these could be useful," he says.

A young guy with a headful of red curls, and a skimpy goatee comes over, and a name tag that reads "Colin" hanging crooked on the left side of his chest strolls over.

"I can let you have that for twenty percent off," he says. He has that perpetually burned-out slowness to his voice that reminds me of Seth Rogen. "In fact, everything in the store is discounted. Not much of any use left, but you might find something."

Nick lowers the bat. "Any ideas? We were at Home Depot and it was a madhouse."

The carrot-topped Colin shrugs. "We already had the madhouse moment. A couple of days ago. Now, we're picked clean and down to three workers who aren't sick and still willing to show up. We probably won't open Monday."

My stomach clenches up. Maybe this is the end of the world. Businesses are closing. The people who are still healthy are afraid to leave the house.

We're at the mall in November and there's no Christmas decorations. The few Halloween decorations that were put up are still there.

I catch Audrey and Nick exchanging glances. Then she steps forward and tosses her hair in a way that makes guys fall all over themselves to be near her. Of course, that's before they find out she's a total bitch.

"Are you sure there's nothing here we can use? Maybe some of that camping food or some kind of container. Batteries? Our dad will be angry if we come back empty-handed."

Audrey could win an Oscar for best actress. Another thing she is better at than I am—lying.

But it works.

"Come on," Colin says. "There are a few things left in the back. We started hoarding stuff a couple of weeks ago, but since some of us never showed back up, I'm guessing they won't be needing it, now."

We follow Colin, his love handles giggling under his red uniform polo. I notice wearily what appears to be dried blood on the back of his pants leg. I hope it's mud, but in the back of my mind, I know it isn't. Unless you live in a cave, we all have seen something terrible at this point.

I can picture him waiting out the zombie apocalypse with a stack of X-Men comics and a PS4 running on a generator. He doesn't appear very shaken up at the moment, so I see him being fairly happy, sort of like the little man who only wanted time to read in that old episode of Twilight Zone I watched with Dad when the SyFy Channel ran that marathon last Fourth of July.

"Why have you even bothered coming back this week?" I ask. "I mean, if nearly everything's gone and nobody's coming in, what's the point?"

Colin pulls a key from his pants and unlocks the door to the storage room. "I don't know why I'm still locking this," he says apologetically. He reaches inside, flips on the lights, and we follow him in.

"I think I was trying to just go on living as normally as I could," he says, "but I stopped going to school a few days ago. I go to Tech part-time, but the last time I went, people were just wandering around on campus. The instructors had stopped coming."

Clothing and shoes scatter the floor of the big room. Nick grabs a lacrosse stick and pretends to play. He makes a raking move and takes off across the room. Colin looks amused. "So, what school do you guys go to?"

"Palmdale High," Audrey tells him, still pretending she's friendly.

Colin shoves his hands deep into his pockets and grins. "Thought so. I could tell by how you're dressed."

"What the heck does that mean?" Audrey snaps, the faux-friendliness instantly gone. She stomps toward the chunky sales guy.

Colin jumps backward. "No offense!" He holds his hands up in front of him. "I meant you all are dressed...kinda rich. I would've figured you guys would be safe from...all this."

Audrey sighs. "We don't dress rich. Our parents are too tight with money."

"Audrey. C'mon." My sister's mental age varies from day to day. Today she's hovering between twelve and fourteen. Looking at Colin, I say, "Nobody's safe."

Colin moves deeper into the starkly lit room. "Listen. Take what you think you can use. I doubt you'll find much, anyhow. Just keep your mouths shut about it. Okay?"

He makes his way toward the door. "Just don't make it obvious. If anyone else is in the store when you're finished, just come through the checkout. Hand me your card, but I won't run it."

Actually, the storage room turns out to be a treasure box, if you consider a camp stove, a hunting bow with a half-dozen arrows, and a couple of collapsible water containers of treasure. Audrey tries on hiking boots and I grab up a couple of sets of Cold Gear long underwear for each of us, guessing at the sizes. It's already cold at night and as I said, I hate cold. If the power goes off for any time, I certainly don't want to sit around shivering to death.

From behind a tall set of shelves, Nick calls out. "Check it out!" He bursts from behind the wall of boxes holding a small black device over his head victoriously.

Audrey looks up from her stacks of boots. "What the hell's that?"

"A hand crank radio." Nick comes closer. "See?" He turns the crank a couple of times and then begins probing the dial. Static and more static and finally he zeroes in on some windbag talk radio host.

"...blame your liberal, do-nothing government. When you watch your children die and your spouse become something ... not human, blame—"

Nick snaps it off. "What an asshole," he mutters. "Anyway, it works. And I might come in useful."

He gives it to me. "Tell your dad he owes me," he says, winking. My heart quickens and I smile, feeling silly.

Audrey remains in her own little world. "I wonder if there are any cool bathing suits back here."

Nick and I look at each other, then burst out laughing.

"Are you sure you need to waste time looking for a new bathing suit?" I ask as Audrey vanishes into the back part of the room.

She rummages through a box labeled Roxy, tossing stringy bras and panties this way and that until she finds one that appeals to her. It's a cute pink number that I could never pull off considering my muscular legs and my lack of curves. "I can use it in the spring. By then things will be back to normal."

I have to like her optimism, if nothing else.

A pair of long men's board shorts hit me in the chest.

"There. I found something for you, too." She cackles as I jerk around to see if Nick heard.

If he did, he does a good job of not laughing.

Batteries are still a no-go, but for some reason, I'm inclined to grab a box of JackLinks Beef Jerky. That stuff's too salty for my tastes, but it's a good source of protein, according to Dad. I sincerely hope I'll never become that desperate for protein.

We leave Dick's Sporting Goods, Nick pushing a cart with our few items—the hand crank radio, Audrey's fabulous new bathing suit, the big barrel bat, the jerky, the thermal underwear, and the case of Powerade (yellow—my favorite!).

He exchanges Instagram handles with Colin, although in all likelihood they'll never contact each other again, and we leave. Colin doesn't bother going through the motions of ringing us up.

I grab a Nike Pink-for-the-Cure soccer ball on the way out and juggle it on my knees as we enter the deserted mall. I try not to think of what might happen to Colin. It's stupid to worry about a person I knew for all of forty-five minutes. But he seems like a smart guy. Nerds don't get enough credit for what they know about surviving—bullies, zombies, or bitchy high school cheerleaders.

Muzak plays over the intercom, too loud against the silence that hangs like a fog.

"I could learn to live like this," Audrey says.

"No, you couldn't," I tell her. "Who would you try to impress?" The ball strikes my insole wrong and bounces away. I jog after it and dribble it back to Audrey and Nick, deftly avoiding the defending benches and trash cans.

"I don't need to impress anyone, Cindy. Why should I bother with people, anyway? Most of them are shit, I told you."

I cut a look at Nick and he rolls his eyes. He's heard the "people are shit" routine before.

"Maybe so, Audrey, but it's better than being alone," Nick says. "The world needs people. People need people."

Audrey refuses to relent completely. "Well, maybe not so many."

I look down the length of the mall toward Sears. The gate is pulled down. There isn't another person in sight between here and there.

"Well, I guess that gets you off the hook, Audrey. No more boring stores." I bounce the ball a couple more times on one knee and then the other, then volley it as hard as I can. That's one thing I can add to my ever-growing list of things I've never done until the zombie apocalypse—kind of a soccer ball the length of Palmdale Mall.

Amazingly, Audrey doesn't mention going to A.E. or any other store. Instead, we head for the Bed Bath and Beyond entrance. I wonder if Dad will be disappointed that we're returning with so few things on the list. Last week's trip was better—Audrey's list of bleach, tampons, toilet paper, and whatnot. It turns out that Dollar General is the place to go for those things. Even more so, because there's a good chance Audrey might die of shame if anyone sees her going in or coming out of a discount store.

Lost in my own thoughts, I move ahead of Nick and the cart and start to push open the door, before realizing a Shambler is standing just outside. Instinctively, we all jump back although it's obvious this newbie has already lost the ability to open or close a door.

It's a boy, about thirteen years old. His surfer blond hair hangs just below his ears, streaked with dried blood. His tanned skin has given way to the gray complexion that accompanies death. His pale blue Reef hoodie is filthy, one sleeve torn off. His thin legs jut out from his wide-legged shorts like a pair of twigs, and what appears to be the whitish glint of bone shows through from the shin to the knee of one leg. He's lost a flip-flip, and the other one sits sideways on his foot, barely hooked at the toes.

Pulling his lips back in what might be mistaken for a grin, he pounds the glass. Faintly, we hear him grunting like an animal struggling to get at its next meal.

"This sucks," Nick whispers like it matters if the Shambler hears him.

We freeze, watching the spastic movements of the boy as he slams the doors with his open hands. He presses his face to the glass, squashing his nose and mouth, smearing blood and snot, and snaps his jaws open and closed as though he might devour us through the window.

"Looks familiar," Audrey says.

"That's because he looks like any of us," Nick replies.

The surfer boy's eyes hold nothing behind them, his expression totally blank. Audrey places her hand on the glass and he lunges at her, his mouth greedily working.

She drums her fingers, t*ap, tap, tap,* like she's teasing a fish inside an aquarium. The boy rams his face against the window, desperate to take a bite of her hand, breaking off one of his perfect front teeth in the process.

"Ew!" Nick and I cry in unison.

"Don't tease them. I ain't proper to tease the dead," comes a scolding voice from behind us. This time all three of us jump. A wizened old woman wearing a black beanie cap, a woolen plaid wrap, and sporting a couple-days growth of stubble on her chin scowls at us for what seems like an eternity. Then she scuttles away, a heavy-looking reusable shopping bag hanging swinging from the end of each arm.

"Stupid thing," Audrey says. I'm not sure if she's referring to the Shambler or the old woman.

Nick sighs. Backing the shopping cart up, he turns and heads toward the next exit, only a few stores down. He looks troubled and I know what he's thinking. It's the same thing I'm thinking.

That kid could've been any of us.

Exiting the mall, we scan the parking lot for more infected. There's nobody out there—dead or alive. We double back to the car and Audrey stands watch, holding the bat as Nick and I load our skimpy loot.

In silence, we drive back toward our end of town. Audrey, taking advantage of the lack of traffic and cops, keeps the needle hovering at seventy all the way home.

CHAPTER 10

◆

November 10
Cindy

The world's going to shit around us, but our little corner of the apocalypse seems almost immune. We go to school, we date (if we're lucky), we play soccer. We're learning to look around the corner of the house and notice how people move as they approach.

Sure, things have changed and have become altered, but we're quickly growing used to armed guards and talks of martial law, and worse—we've grown accustomed to the curfews. In a matter of a couple of months, the N-Virus has become a part of everyday life and so have the Shamblers.

Sometimes when I watch the news or log onto the internet, I catch the headlines and feel sort of guilty. But everything has a way of balancing out.

I've heard Audrey say, "Karma's a bitch" more times than I can count. It's her little method of excusing herself for not caring what happens to other people.

Maybe she's right for once.

Sometimes I'm just waiting for our safe little existence to break apart.

Some say memories are like ghosts. But maybe they're like snakes, too. They lay low almost forgotten, and then they strike when you're least expecting it. Tonight will be the latter. It'll be a snake coiled in the back of my mind, waiting to sink its fangs in for the rest of my life.

My phone buzzes and I'm surprised to see it's Audrey.

"Listen, need Mom or Dad to come and pick me up," Audrey says before I can say anything. Her phone keeps going in and out and for a moment, she sounds like she's calling from the bottom of a bucket.

"Are you okay?" I ask.

Dad and Mom are both looking at me. Parents have that exquisite sixth sense when it comes to their kids, I've discovered.

"Just come. I'm fine."

The realization dawns on Dad's face before Mom and I understand. She's been in an accident, maybe. Bruises. Lacerations. Shit, a missing limb is better than what I know is coming.

The simple piercing of the skin with a set of infected teeth and our little protected world fell apart. We've just lost one of our four wheels.

She'd been out with Tommy Barker. Tommy is a stupid pseudo-hoodlum with a rich mother, richer grandparents, and a dad who's famous for some reality show from five years ago. The dad isn't present and the mom's only around when it comes to opening her checkbook.

We rush out of the door, to Mom's SUV together like a weird three-headed being.

"I thought she was at the library," Mom says, her voice too shrill. It sounds like an accusation. She goes to the driver's side door, but Dad takes the keys from her shaking hands.

"I'd better drive, Meg."

We pile in, the tires squealing as Dad tears out of the driveway.

"I dropped her at the library. I was going back to get her at ten," Mom jabbers. She's on the verge of crying, trying to hold it in. "They have armed escorts to and from the building."

In the backseat, I want to throw up. I knew what she was up to. And no, she didn't tell me. I just knew. Maybe it's that universal part of being a teenager—knowing how to lie. I can see her pointing out Tommy Barker sitting in his stupid raised pickup truck at the far end of the parking area. She'd tell the armed escort that he's her brother. Maybe the escort won't buy it, but he also doesn't care as long as he gets these kids and these old farts in and out of the library without being devoured by some crazed lunatic. Then he can go home at the closing with a clear conscious.

I wish I could have a clear conscious. I should've told. She would've hated me a little more intensely than usual for a couple of days, but that would be okay. She'd get over it.

She isn't getting over this. Nobody will.

I smell death—it permeates the entire E.R. and I try to breathe through my mouth as I make my way past the gurneys of sick patients that line the walls of the corridor. I don't miss this place at all. Maybe that desire to be a doctor died right along with all those other stupid notions about a normal future.

Inside the waiting area, there are more people—some of whom appear they're battling the common flu, which is common with the N-Virus, others looking like they've come from the losing end of a war zone. A young woman holds a little boy of about six in her lap, his arm wrapped in a blood-soaked t-shirt. Her eyes are wide and dry, and her mouth looks like she's biting back a scream. Another woman, her mother, I assume—they look very much alike—holds the young mother's hand. The older woman's face is so tired. Tired of what life has recently become.

"… just came up into the backyard, like he always does after school. Robbie let him inside the gate. They always play together. He didn't look any different until I saw his eyes…"

I hear enough. An old man leans against a metal walking cane, blood pooling around his feet. Just below the knee, a wet gash glints through the tatters of his pants leg. He'll be left to die out here. They'll take those who have "connections" in first.

Lucky for Audrey. Not so lucky for some of the others, I suppose. I feel bad about that, but that's life. I mentioned something to that effect a few nights ago, and Dad reminded me that these are different times. We have to take our advantages and use them as best we can.

Families are dying. We have to make sure it's other families—not ours.

"Better them than us." Audrey said that on more than one occasion since the N-Virus became the latest CNN headline.

I'm allowed to go through—Mom's already back there, but I stay in the waiting room to phone Grandma. That's my way of avoiding this. For a few more moments, at least, I want us to not be other families.

A couple of nurses nod and shoot me this solemn-faced look as I pass. Audrey's sitting on the gurney looking glassy-eyed and stupid, hair a mess, her designer jeans and blouse a mess of dirt. Dark splotches decorate her pale jeans, but there's not much blood, no more than what you'd get if you cut yourself shaving your legs.

Mom's eyes nearly pinched shut from crying, but she's just sitting there now, red-faced, red-eyed, with makeup-like bruises. Her hands twist in her lap like she doesn't know what to do with them.

I'm tentative and Dad can tell. "I gave her a sedative. Just in case..." He doesn't need to finish. We've seen victims change, some within a matter of moments. It's been roughly forty-eight minutes since Audrey's call. We have no idea how long it's been since she was bitten.

Dad's already cleaned and dressed the wound and is tidying up. "Didn't need stitches. Wasn't much of a bite. Maybe the exposure was minimal," he says, mostly to himself.

"Not much of a bite?" Audrey asks, her words slurring like Mom's do after a couple of glasses of wine. "Bastard wrecked my best jeans." She sticks out her wounded leg and sways on the gurney. I reach out to steady her.

Mom doesn't move. She's suddenly afraid to touch my sister.

I haven't believed in miracles since I was eight. When I was younger, I used to think they happened, but as I've grown older, I've discovered miracles are exceedingly rare and saved for a privileged few.

I saw that when Grandpa got sick. I kept believing—praying, he would get better. I just knew he would. But he just got sicker and sicker. Eventually, I convinced myself that my grandpa had run away and had been replaced with a hideous, pitiful skeleton man who lived in a hospital room. When I visited, I acted as if he was a stranger.

He died without me telling him goodbye.

But that was then.

This is now.

Dad leads us to his office, away from the noise, the chatter, and weeping of the E.R. Mom's hysteria has become a quiet thing, and Audrey is still loopy from the sedative. I'm in a disconnected sort of stupor, half-expecting to wake at any moment.

Dad closes the door and locks it. He walks over to his desk without a word, removes his keys from his pants pocket, and unlocks one of the drawers.

Removing a trio of small unlabeled vials, he finally speaks. "I have this experimental vaccine. It's called Phalanx, and it's worked in a few cases, so far." He takes a hypodermic syringe from his lab coat, rips open the wrapper, and fills it with the clear liquid from one of the vials.

"Where'd you get this?" Mom asks, her voice shaking.

"I just have it." He moves over to Audrey and swabs her arm with an alcohol gauze. "No mention of this outside this room." Audrey doesn't flinch when Dad jabs the needle into her bicep.

Dad glances at me and winks. "Now, let's cross our fingers that this will work."

Against everything I've learned and know, feel myself starting to believe again. Smiling, I cautiously take Audrey's hand and squeeze her cool fingers.

Audrey searches the empty air, before focusing on my face. What a space cadet. "You're so weird," she says and giggles softly.

CHAPTER 11

November 13
Nick

Sometimes the light doesn't go on until something hits you dead in the face.

I'm watching the world change around me and for some reason, I feel nothing. In the corner, Mom and Grandma chat about things that no longer matter—some long out-of-touch cousin, whom they married or divorced or some shit like that —and all I want to do is scream at them, "Why the fuck are you wasting your last few hours like this?"

Outside, rain patters softly against the windows. The day's a dreary shade of gray that makes you want to stay in your room and pretend you're the only one alive.

I shouldn't have said that. Soon, I might not have to pretend.

Grandma was attacked late yesterday, right on her front porch as she stepped out to get the mail. She broke the news to Mom over the phone. I couldn't tell if Mom wanted to scream or weep or just pass out. Instead, she just sank to the kitchen floor. But her voice remained unchanged. She could've been discussing a new recipe or something they saw on television. I have to hand it to her—she managed it better than I could've imagined. Especially after the shitty way she handled Dad's death.

Still, the look on her face is one of those stupid, horrible moments that I'll always remember. I froze and waited for her to get off the phone, but I already knew what had happened.

"It was the little girl from next door," Grandma told her over the phone.

Mom and Grandma never got along very well—there was always some petty little weight hanging over them, the rope ready to break any moment. Tension forced pleasantries. Aunt Sara was always Grandma's favorite—that much was obvious, but Aunt Sara says she can't come back for this.

Four hundred miles is a long drive to watch someone die, I suppose. Especially when people are dying all around you. Dying's not special anymore.

Grandma's house is just like it always was. It's just like you'd think a grandma's house should be if you live in the South. Immaculate lawn with a jungle of azaleas, dripping with hot-pink blooms in spring, but rather skeletal now that fall has set in and the lawn maintenance people have stopped coming. Diseased patches of grass have gone brown from lack of care. At the far end of the backyard looms a magnolia, taller than the roof of the two-story house, the gnarled limbs like the arms of an old buddy. I spent many hours in those limbs, nearly cradled, loving the perfume of the white flowers and the feel of the sturdy, waxy leaves in my fingers.

Inside the house, floral-patterned drapes create splashes of color that are offset by an elegant beige sofa that children under the age of fifteen aren't allowed to sit on. Dark wood tables polished to a high shine. On a shelf, there's a framed photo of a grandfather I never knew, but everyone says I resemble. Not a speck of dirt anywhere; shoes are left at the door. Never a pet to leave its mark or shed its fur.

Music plays softly, some classical piano stuff I can't identify. It all sounds the same to me. The air smells of Lysol and potpourri, both serving to disguise something bad.

The bad smell is Grandma. It hit me hard enough to make my throat close up when we first got here and I went to kiss her.

Earlier, Mom and Grandma baked some cookies and then made a pan of Baklava— the old family came from Greece and recipes are all that's left to prove it. Then they looked through boxes of old jewelry, Grandma passing along little stories about where this pair of earrings came from or what year Granddad gave her that ring or necklace. After the jewelry, came the books of photos.

"Look at you, Nicky," Grandma said, her sweet voice growing creakier by the moment. "I used to hold you for hours." With a trembling hand, she touches my hair. I almost flinch away, but catch myself. No matter what, she's Grandma until the end.

Until her eyes grow white and her face grows angry.

We go into Grandma's bedroom.

"Get that box down from that shelf, Nicky," she says, motioning toward her closet. I do and it's actually several shoeboxes stacked inside a larger file box. Mom and Grandma sit on the bed and begin going through them, removing envelopes, folded papers that look important or at least official, and clippings from newspapers.

"I always wanted to get around to organizing these things. I was too busy keeping the part of the house that everyone saw tidy. I never worried about old papers."

I sit on the floor next to the bed and remember crawling up under the bed and hiding from my cousin, Joe. It feels like a hundred years ago. Mom says Joe, a month younger than me, was bitten a couple of weeks ago, but she doesn't know anything more.

I haven't seen Joe since we were twelve and now I imagine him still as twelve, lumbering around, drooling, bloody, and snarling.

Miles did take a moment to console Mom and make arrangements. Everything is ready for the "big moment."

There are armed "transition directors" outside the house. At the end of the driveway is a van that looks like a prisoner transport, but instead of "police" the sides are emblazoned with "The Pastures," in fancy gold letters, hovering above rolling hills that are so bright green it makes my eyes ache.

The number is 1-888-DIGNITY.

Everything is commercial. Even the end of the world.

November 14
Cindy

I decide to take a run, against Mom's wishes. If she has it her way, I doubt I'll be allowed to leave the house at all, except to go to school. Especially after Audrey's deal. I tell myself that she's just gone to a friend's home; that she's fine.

It's better to think that way than to allow bad thoughts in.

So, I plug my iPod into my ears, my heart thudding like a bass drum in my head just before I press play. I miss the four-times-a-week soccer practices, and cross country isn't happening due to the danger, but I need running for release. Even more, I need the time to just allow my mind to go blank.

There are three boys, maybe ten years old, teasing a Shambler at the lesser-used entrance of our neighborhood. I recognize one—it's Noel Freeman, a chunky little piece of work whose dad is a county councilman. His sister, Jenna, is in Audrey's class, but, believe it or not, she's too bitchy and snooty for Audrey. Mrs. Freeman is one of those moms who always wears an expression that can make you feel like you've done something wrong even if you haven't.

Either way, county councilman is the smallest amount of power I've ever seen go to anyone's head.

The Shambler is wearing tan coveralls with the legend "Palmdale Water and Sewer" emblazoned on the back. When he turns around, his front is a bloody mess where something has gotten at him and relieved him of most of his vital organs. His formerly dark complexion has gone the color of modeling clay. Noel and one other kid are whacking at this man with golf clubs, and I'm happy that all I can hear is the thin, mechanical sound of FeverRay and their shallow but mesmerizing music. I keep on running. I don't care about those kids any more than I do the Shambler. If he takes a chunk out of one of them, so be it. They're asking for it, anyway.

CHAPTER 12

November 15
Nick

How is a person supposed to react to seeing zombies being maintained in a green field surrounded by an electric fence? How is a person supposed to react to seeing his grandmother in that field?

We board a bus that reminds me too much of the transport bus that carries tourists from the Disney hotels to the parks—crowded with stupid-faced people (and maybe they think I'm stupid-faced, too) kids who are crying too much, handicapped people, old people who look so helpless that I can't stand to look at them.

It's stuffy in here and smells of B.O. and illness. I stand, holding onto an overhead strap, having given up my seat to an overweight woman who says her brother is out there and "waiting to see her."

I nod and let her sag into the seat beside Mom. Mom smiles a tight smile like she's proud that I'm being a gentleman when I know in her heart she doesn't give a shit.

We start away, the bus's engine wheezing, my mind drifting to things even more useless than this. Audrey. Why should I even care what happens to her? But part of me does. Even stranger, I find myself thinking of Cindy. How's Cindy doing? Cindy called the morning after Audrey was attacked. She knew Tommy would tell everything because Tommy Barker was a piece of shit. She wouldn't tell me anything other than Audrey should be okay. They'd know in a few days.

A few days?

The N-Virus has an incubation period of only a few hours, according to the news reports, so that's weird in itself.

Worse than that, Audrey was cheating on me with that guy? Now, I have to wonder what a loser I must be.

Somewhere in the darkest parts of my brain and my heart, I want to see Audrey out there in the Pastures. I would have her trade places with Grandma in a moment. Grandma never lied to me. Audrey made lying to me a habit.

The fields are this insane, fake-looking green, like a photo that has been digitally enhanced. It's too fucking tranquil.

I don't notice the television monitors hanging in the front and the rear of the shuttle until they flash to life.

A male announcer comes on-screen, looking so polished and perfect that he might be digitally enhanced, as well. In a deep, but sympathetic tone he begins his pitch.

"Welcome to the most humane way to handle the transformation of your loved ones. The Pastures provide the care you crave for your partially departed as they enter the final decline. View and visit in the safety and comfort of our top-of-the-line shuttle transports. Purchase the dual package, which includes transformation pasture space and final cremation, and get a 15 percent discount. Most insurance plans accepted and payment plans available."

What a waste. The creep reminds me of those hypocritical preachers that come on late at night to empty the pockets of gullible old people. "For a $100 donation, I'll be sure to include your name on my prayer list tonight." Give me a break.

The shuttle rounds a sharp turn and someone nearer the front gasps. Everyone starts shuffling around, getting to their feet, elbowing through to get a good look through the barred windows.

There they are—Shamblers staggering around in ultra-clean green grass fields, wearing what they died (the first time) in. An old man in loose pants and a bloody shirt lurches along, arms outstretched, head waggling like he's raging at something only he sees. His white hair billows out in the breeze like dingy cotton. A woman begins weeping, loud and wet, and a man mutters to her, something comforting, I assume.

I look at Mom, who stares straight ahead. I wonder if she really needs to see Grandma like this. I don't want my memories of my lovely, funny grandmother reduced to this—something out of the *Dawn of the Dead.*

"Can we stop for a moment?" a grandfatherly man asks. He's seated midway back and starts toward the front of the bus.

Another man, dressed in a dark suit with a white carnation on the lapel stands, his hands up. "Sir, I need to ask you to take your seat."

"My wife…" the older man says.

"Who the hell is that guy?" a middle-aged guy says. He's flabby enough to burst out of his pink Lactose golf shirt.

"I'm the funeral director, sir," the dark-suited man answers. "I'm afraid we cannot stop. Please view through the side windows."

The guy looks a lot more like a cop than a funeral director, with his buzz cut and wide chest. More than that, the gun belt that peeks out from beneath his jacket when he moves is a dead giveaway.

"This is just like the fuckin' Kilimanjaro Safari at Disney World," the flabby golfer mutters. His wife places her hand on his thick bicep and he quiets.

The old gentleman returns to his seat looking defeated. He watches a woman that could be my own Grandmother through the window, her gray hair crazy, and her pale blue dress covered in filth. A tear rolls down his wrinkled cheek and I look away.

The funeral director/cop guy eyes the golfer dude, way too anxious to make a move on him.

As we rounded the next easy turn, I saw her. My lovely, beautiful grandmother. The woman who kissed my knees when I wrecked them on my skateboard and made cookies even when mom said I couldn't eat sweets. Out there in the Pastures like a fucking animal.

She turns, alerted by the rumbling growl of the bus, and stares our way, not really seeing through her white eyes. Her head jerks from side to side like she's having some sort of fit. Her lips are drawn back, exposing her large, perfect dentures and I wonder why they won't remove the teeth of the infected that are being kept in a "living" state.

She limps toward the electric fence, barefooted. I guess she wasn't wearing shoes when she changed.

I can no longer bear seeing this. Mom removes a tissue from her purse and dabs the corners of her eyes. I put my hand on her shoulder and she looks up, forcing another small, exhausted smile.

"At least she's not suffering," she says.

I nod. But I wonder if that's the case. Do they not feel anything? If so, why not just let them go quickly, in case there's some sort of afterlife waiting for them?

CHAPTER 13

November 18
Cindy

I need to stop eavesdropping. It used to be a comforting thing, listening to my parents chatting about their day in the waning hours of the evening. Pleasant things, sometimes things that were inappropriate to share with a couple of teenage daughters (and let me make this clear—I never listened to them doing anything but talking. I'm guessing that's why iPods were invented.) But since the N-Virus, there hasn't been any pleasant talk coming from their bedroom. Things are spiraling downward and it's going so fast, Dad isn't going to be able to stop it. I used to think Dad was Superman. Now I know he's just a regular guy trying to hold his shit together. Trying to hold us all together.

He believes he failed Audrey although he managed to get his hands on the vaccine. Mom thinks so, too, although she tries to hide it. She's always been shitty at hiding things. You'd think a real estate broker would be able to lie better than that. She should at least try. For his sake. But I can hear it in her voice. There's disappointment hidden in her words.

Or maybe it's my imagination.

"The vaccine seems to be working. Maybe we caught it in time," Dad says.

"Can you get more, do you think? Will she need more? What if one of us needs it, too?" Mom questions.

"Don't worry. I've cashed in everything," Dad tells her. "The college funds. I've cashed in our life insurance policies. Our retirement. I'm getting another drop in two days."

The college funds. My heart breaks. This thing just keeps getting more and more real. It's so real that even college is no longer a priority. The world is ending. Otherwise, Dad and Mom would never touch our college money.

"Is this going to devastate us?" Mom asks. It sounds like she is crying a little.

Dad doesn't respond for a couple of moments. Finally, he says, "How can it devastate us? We'll all be alive and together. That's more than a lot of people are getting. Besides, it'll buy us time. There could be an actual cure in a matter of weeks. We just have to hang in there." He pauses and I imagine him kissing Mom in the middle of her forehead like he sometimes does. Like he's kissing the worry away. "Just a little longer."

All Dad wants is for us to be alive and together. Has it gotten to that? Have things gotten so real and horrible that simply being uninfected is the most important thing in the world?

I move away from the wall and go downstairs for a glass of milk. When I flip on the kitchen lights, Audrey's there, sitting at the table, in the dark. I jump like an idiot.

"Holy crap, Audrey. What are you doing?"

"Don't feel very good," she says. "I keep drinking water, but I'm still so thirsty."

"I don't feel so great, either," I tell her, thinking about our now nonexistent college funds.

I take out the plastic jug of milk and pour up a half-glass, finishing it up. That's it—all the milk and I wonder if we'll be able to get more. Shipments of fresh foods to the nearest Food Lion have been more infrequent. A world without a cold glass of milk would suck.

It's the little things, you know. Milk. Fresh apples. Maybe we can move into the country, get away from everyone, and farm.

I sit down across from my sis. She does look sick. Her skin is sallow and it looks like bruises beneath her eyes. Maybe it's the fluorescent lights, but in any light, Audrey's never looked less than ready for a photo shoot.

"Maybe it's the vaccine," I offer. "Could be some sort of side effect."

She gulps more water, leaving oily smears on the side of her glass. "Probably. Either way, I think I'll skip school tomorrow."

"I doubt anyone will notice," I say, meaning a lot of people are skipping school lately.

"Speak for yourself, little sis. I'm the reason people come to school," Audrey says, but even her tried and true conceit comes out so hollow that I can't come up with a decent retort.

We sit there a little longer and something gnaws at me. It's like everything I do with my family is for the last time. I keep Dad and Mom's conversation to myself.

November 19
Cindy

Audrey has no idea Tommy snapped a shot of her mangled leg with his iPhone and posted it to Instagram. When I got to school on Monday, everyone already knew what had happened. The only question is, has Audrey turned?

I stop Nick in the hallway on the way to First Period, but he has already gotten the lowdown in homeroom. I'm not sure what the driving part of the story is—that Audrey has been bitten or that she's cheated on Nick.

Nick doesn't seem to be surprised. In fact, he's strangely calm.

"You know, I'm around. If you want to talk," I tell him.

"Not much to talk about, is there?" he says with a shrug that tells me he's hurt and trying to hide it.

"I don't know. Is there?" I ask. I glance around, thinking people might be trying to listen, but the halls are quiet. There's about a third of the student body there this morning. Every day it grows thinner. Are all these people sick or dead or in-between?

Nick pushes his hair back from his beautiful face. "Okay. We'll get together later. At the field."

I nod and start away, but he grabs my arm. "Wait, Cindy."

"Yeah?"

"She not...one of them, is she?"

"No."

Not yet.

After school, I find Nick sitting on the highest bleacher alone. The wind blusters his hair widely and he looks like a boy from one of those magazines. Except for his expression—mouth a tight line, jaw clenched. He waves and I come up, not especially graceful.

"I thought we'd have a better chance if a Shambler discovers us out here. I haven't seen one who can climb very well," he says.

"Seen a lot of them lately, I assume?"

"More than I want to see. My grandma turned last week."
The tone of his voice gives away nothing, but his throat
works hard like he's holding in a sob. Or a scream.

I touch his hand. "I'm so sorry, Nick. I had no idea."

"Someone getting the N-Virus is hardly big news lately.
They sent her over to the Pastures. They said it would be
fine, but it was horrible. Those poor people. They're
monsters. They've become monsters and they're keeping
them around just to pacify the living." He squeezes my hand
back and his blue eyes glisten with tears when he looks at
me.

"I'm still having nightmares," he whispers. "Is Audrey like
that?"

"No. No!" I tell him. "Not at all."

"Why? She was bitten, according to that asshole. I saw
the photo—he sent it to me like he was proud or something."

"Well, she's okay." Part of me wants to tell him that she
wasn't bitten—it's all a joke. A bad, tasteless fucking joke and
he's the target. Teenagers aren't above that sort of behavior,
you know, but I can't lie to him again. "She was bitten, but
she hasn't contracted the N-Virus."

"How?"

"I can't tell you that."

"You have to," Nick says. "I need to know she's not going
to be one of those things."

"Nick..."

"Tell me, Cindy."

"Why does it matter, anyway? She cheated on you with a douchebag. You shouldn't even care what happens to her."

"I don't know why," Nick nearly shouts, staring straight ahead now rather than looking at me. "Audrey has always been ... above it all. Above us. She's sorta untouchable, you know? If this gets her, it will get us all."

I nod. He made his case. "My dad was able to get an experimental vaccine. It seems to be working."

Nick smiles. "So there's hope for those of us who are left."

"There's always hope. We just can't give up."

I grab my backpack and pull out my lunch bag. Mom made up her famous "funky-chunky chicken salad," which is usually fresh avocado, roasted chicken, and whatever else she deems worthy of being included in her gourmet delicacy, stuffed into a whole wheat pita. Today, it's canned chicken and pre-packaged guacamole. Not exactly inedible, but not the same, either. I offer Nick half. He takes it, mutters a thanks, and takes a hearty bite.

"Not bad," he said. "Better than mystery meat."

Agreeing, I remove two bottles of water from the bag next and hand him one. We sit, eating in silence in a row on bleachers that overlook an overgrown soccer field that may never be used again. Overhead, white clouds float by like fat ghosts. The sun is like a caress, a reminder that summer and normalcy are only a few months behind us. There are no sounds around us. I find myself missing the low chaos of track practice or football practice or even cheerleading. Band practice is canceled for the time being, so the missed notes on the trombone no longer echo from the music room, followed by Mr. Wigg's bitchy comments. Nice one, Leslie. Now try and play the song the rest of the band is playing, how about it? Yes, I even miss that.

The constant hum of traffic on the highway beyond the fields is now only a whisper. Looking up, I spot a lone aircraft that appears to be some sort of military jet. My heart jumps in behind my ribs, but I don't say anything to Nick.

I hadn't felt like eating at lunch and opted for the seclusion of the library instead. I can still access the Internet regularly there. At home, the connection has become iffy so I've missed things—those "secret" things that aren't covered by the cable news networks. Apparently, our dear president/dictator/whatever decided it'll be a good idea to send as many Shamblers to their final death as possible by drone-bombing a particularly afflicted part of Detroit this morning.

I wonder if they made provisions for the uninfected to get out first. My gut is telling me no. Could they decide to do that sort of thing to Palmdale?

Phalanx is probably pretty easy to get if you're the President of the United States. He doesn't even have to buy it illegally.

We sit out there a while longer. Nick removes his pad from his satchel and sketches a fairy with transparent dragonfly wings and my face. I blush because that's my standard reaction around Nick Thatcher.

Just as he's shading in the shadows beneath Fairy Cindy's ample breast (thanks, Nick!), someone calls, "You kids need to get yourselves home!" We both glance up, startled. There's a security guard standing at the bottom of the bleachers. "I don't want to tell you more than once. You know it's dangerous these days."

"It is getting late," I say, stuffing the wads of wax paper and used napkins back into my lunch bag.

"You need a ride?" Nick asks.

I shake my head. "I brought Audrey's car."

Just before I start away, he tears out the drawing of the Fairy Cindy and gives it to me. "Be careful," he says. He jogs toward his Jeep on the other side of the parking area before I can respond.

CHAPTER 14

November 24
Cindy

It's been two weeks since Audrey was bitten. Dad's put all the money we have into those black market Phalanx vaccines. But Audrey's hanging in there. We're all hanging in there, I suppose. Dad's at the hospital almost around the clock, now. Sometimes he sleeps there. He's kept the knowledge of the vaccine to himself, and I've shared it with nobody but Nick, who'll keep it to himself. Everyone else who has been exposed to the virus has become a Shambler within a matter of hours.

Mom makes a showing of working, immersing herself in her office here at home, NPR playing soft in the background, a little jazz, a little classical, and too much bad news. People just aren't into buying and selling real estate right now, she says, as if she needs to make excuses for the lack of business.

She drinks too much wine in the evening—the cases of the expensive red she bought at some auction to bring out only when we have "special" company is nearly gone. The boxes are empty and the few bottles left are tucked into the wine chiller beneath the kitchen counter.

She's going to be in a hell of a fix when she runs out completely. Going to the supermarket is a bitch already. People are stocking more and more, supermarket shipments are irregular and usually garbage nobody wants to eat. I can tell you I'm sick and tired of Tuna Helper and Ragu Spaghetti. But we have enough of that kind of shit to last at least a year, so there's no way we're going to starve—unless it's by choice.

With Audrey making an appearance at school at least a couple of times, and popping up on Instagram and FaceTime (in low lighting—she still looks less than perfect), rumors are swirling that it's Tommy Barker who lied.

We're both getting more satisfaction from that than we probably should.

Still, something's going on with Big Sis. She's not the same. Dad says it is probably some sort of side effect—the vaccine is untested, so we don't know what to expect. But I'm afraid it's something worse. Maybe the vaccine just isn't working. Sure, it's slowed things down, but something's still happening.

I think Audrey is turning.

I know that same thought is lying at the back of Dad's mind, too. He's just too afraid of saying it. Saying it makes it a reality.

December 1
Cindy

Thanksgiving break came and went without a lot of
fanfare. Dad made the trip across town to pick up Grandma.
She made her pumpkin pie, but something wasn't quite right
with it this year. Later, she admitted that she resorted to
using applesauce instead of fresh eggs since she couldn't get
her hands on any. Of course, we all ate it and pretended it
was as great as it always was. There was no turkey, but Dad
did get his hands on a canned ham, so we ate it, and then the
two of us lounged around in the den reading and napping
away the afternoon. Mom and Grandma sat at the kitchen
table, talking too softly to hear. In the background, a repeat
of last year's Super Bowl played softy, the sounds enough to
help us pretend things are normal.

This year's NFL season had been suspended indefinitely.
In the back of my mind, I wondered how many of those
players, announcers, and fans were infected. Dead?
Somewhere in between?

Mom drank her wine, and later, Dad took Grandma home
(although we all practically begged her to stay with us until
this was over). Then he went to the hospital. Audrey stayed

in her room testing different kinds of foundation to see which ones would cover up her deteriorating complexion.

Nick and I Skyped a computerized drawing of a nerdy kid back and forth, each of us adding scrapes, scars, torn clothing, and blood until we had a proper ubergeek Shambler.

Stupid to make light of such things when Audrey was in the next room, possibly becoming a Shambler herself.

I've never been a big Thanksgiving person, but I missed the cozy blandness of the holiday. I hope by Christmas things will be better.

Back at school, there's a lot of talk about canceling classes until the N-Virus is under control. Hearing this, Audrey has developed a renewed desire to go back, to make an appearance. Outwardly, this seems to be a display of determination and strength. Mom and Dad talk about what a great person she is. An inspiration.

I'm proud of her too, but come on. We're not allowed to speak of the black market supply of Phalanx, so in the eyes of the remaining assholes who crawl the halls of Palmdale High School, Audrey isn't sick and Tommy Barker is full of shit.

I know the real motivation behind Audrey's desire to go to school one last time before it closes. She's going to get back at Tommy somehow. She'll confront him, comment on his tiny penis, or his latent preference for members of the varsity football team. Not especially creative, but nonetheless effective. Audrey has a gift of delivery.

Besides, who the hell knows when they'll be together again, what's left of this year's graduating class?

I'm standing in front of my vanity mirror, twisting my hair into a loose ponytail, when I hear a strange noise from Audrey's bathrooms.

"Blahh!"

That doesn't sound good at all.

Again, all wet sounding, splashing. I wrinkle my nose on impulse and enter Big Sis's bedroom, not really wanting to see anything. I step closer to peek into her bathroom. The door is open just enough for me to see her kneeling on the floor in front of the bowl.

"Are you okay?" I ask.

There's blood staining the rim of the toiler, running down the side like spilled paint, so dark it's almost black. My own stomach does the funky chicken for a moment, and I breathe deep and long to regain control.

"Dynamite. Can't you tell?" Audrey croaks and then heaves again.

"Should I get Mom? Maybe I can catch Dad—" I place my hand on her back, feeling like a very small child because I can't help her. Mentally, I can't stop going over the list of N-Virus symptoms, like a stupid news broadcast in my brain.

The second stage is followed by severe chills, vomiting of blood or other bodily fluid, extreme lethargy…

"N-no. I'll be fine in a few minutes."

"Maybe it's a side effect of the Phalanx," I offer.

Audrey finishes barfing and sits back on the floor. She wipes her mouth with a wad of toilet paper, tosses it in the pot, and flushes. "Get the hell out, Cindy. And don't say a word about this to Mom or Dad."

I shrug and get the hell out as she asks. Ten minutes later, we drive to school in uneasy silence. Although it's supposed to be morning rush hour, the roads aren't crowded, except for olive green military trucks full of soldiers and the two checkpoints with local cops in riot gear between our house and school. Audrey flashes her sexiest smile from behind the wheel and the cops wave us through both times. Most of the restaurants have closed, except for an Italian joint that has steadfastly hung in there for early dinners a few nights a week, turning customers out before curfew.

The supermarket opens for four hours in the afternoons. Office-based businesses have closed. People (like Mom) can work just as well from home, as long as the Internet stays up, plus there's no chance of a rabid co-worker tearing out your throat in the break room.

I have to admit, Audrey looks pretty good. She's done a remarkable job with her makeup and doesn't look the least bit dead. Which, of course, she's not. The rose petal pink blush has given her the necessary glow she needs to appear in good health.

When we pull up at the school, she gives me her best fake-assed beauty queen smile.

"Let's go in and see what these morons have to say," she says, throwing her too-expensive Alexander McQueen bag over her shoulder.

I glance around, still not used to the trio of armed security guards flanking the upper portion of the student parking area. It's a cloudy morning, and seeing these guys dressed out in their bulky gear makes the whole scene feel apocalyptic and hopeless. Audrey is ahead of me, walking like she means business. She vanishes behind the glass doors and is already gone by the time I enter.

The usual hustle and bustle of the morning scramble to homeroom is no longer there. The attendance is sparse—our class sizes have dropped from around twenty on a normal day to about eight or ten. Other classes have lost their teachers and are now combined. Science is one of those. Mrs. Lester stopped coming last week, so her class is now sitting in with Mr. Batson during the Fourth Period. That would be okay, except Mrs. Lester's crowd was full of football dorks doing just enough to get by—something Mr. Batson isn't used to with his group of over-achievers. Most of the time, it's a swirling mess of idle chatter and bathroom humor. Mr. Batson blushes a lot lately, his bald head turning an alarming shade of dark crimson.

Things run smoothly for the first part of the day. There's the ongoing talk of martial law being instituted in Palmdale like it has in the bigger cities. Worse, there's talk that people are being "removed"—uninfected people. I'm not sure it's true, but there are a lot of people I haven't seen in quite a while, from school, from town. Teachers, students. Mom mentioned last night she can't reach three of her most reliable salespeople.

Somehow, thinking our government might be taking people away is much scarier than thinking they are falling ill.

I pass Audrey's locker just before lunch. Someone has written, "Audrey Scott has crotch rote" in huge red letters on the door. Nice. A misspelled insult.

I stop, fumble through my bag for a pen, and try scribbling over it in a black Sharpie. It doesn't do anything but get me in trouble.

"Cindy Scott. You're vandalizing school property!" I look up to see Mr. Warner marching toward me, his face screwed into a stupid scowl.

"I was just..."

He snatches the pen from my hand and leans in close enough for me to smell alcohol on his breath. "I'm assigning you detention, Miss Scott. Effective as soon as we get back to a normal school schedule."

"Sorry, Mr. Warner. But I didn't want my sister to have this on her locker."

"Adding to the defacement doesn't help," he snaps. He starts away without looking back.

Down the hall, Tommy Barker and his little group low-I.Q. jocks laugh, obviously proud of both their clever wit and lack of spelling skills.

I flip them off, which makes them laugh even more, and head to the next period. It's Mr. Carlton's literature class, the highlight of the day. Well, that and catching a peek of Nick's perfect little hiney in those well-worn A.E. jeans as he rushes past. He glances back at me and flashes a tight smile. I wave like a silly little girl and he vanishes through the doors of his next class.

At lunch, I find Brandi and we sit together in the cafeteria. The air is heavy with burned cooking oil. No more eating at the fields, the administration has decided. It's too dangerous with the stray Shamblers wandering Palmdale. So much for fresh air and sunshine. I decided to splurge and buy a sugary Coke and an order of fries, despite the tuna salad Mom packed for me. An unhealthy dose of grease, salt, and sugar can make even the zombie apocalypse almost tolerable. Brandi and I have little to talk about, but it was better than being alone. I can't help but believe every time I see some of these people might be the last time. Morbid, I know.

I notice Audrey's bitch-posse has grown thin. She's sitting with Haley Matthews and Madison Throne, but Brittany Pope hasn't been to school in at least a week. Today was the first time I've noticed her absence. It's terrible to say, but school is more pleasant without some people.

December 3
Cindy

A rare evening with Dad at home. Things feel normal—almost. He cooks for us—tuna casserole. Jesus, I'm sick of canned tuna, canned chicken, and deviled ham. Yuck! Still, somehow, Dad manages to make even tuna casserole taste pretty good—fat egg noodles cooked al dente (Mom always cooks the pasta to mush—sorry, Mom!), cheddar cheese, garlic bread crumbs toasted on top. Maybe he's a magician because it smells good enough to make my stomach rumble like crazy.

We eat in front of the television—something that is usually saved for Friday nights if we're all at home together.

Needless to say, it's been a while since we noshed in style on the sofa and at the coffee table, in front of the tube.

Mom takes the bottle of wine into the family room with her. "White, my dear, to go with the fish," she jokes, making those annoying finger quotations in the air when she says fish. She's been hitting the wine hard since Audrey became ill. Dad plays along with his patented Dad-smile, but when Mom isn't paying attention, he looks at her with so much sadness in his eyes that I want to run to my bedroom and hide my head under the covers.

He feels like a failure because he couldn't protect Audrey. I want to tell him that he can't protect us from ourselves, but tonight I just pretend we're happy and the world is normal.

We watch reruns of The Big Bang Theory and Audrey complains.

"These people are so geeky and lame," she says. "Let's watch Vampire Diaries."

"You can watch Vampire Diaries when your mother and I go to bed," Dad tells her. "Now eat all of your food. You need the calories to battle the virus."

"We have the vaccine, don't we? Why do I need to ruin my bod with this...stuff?" She shovels a gob of casserole on her fork and lets it drop back into her plate. Splat.

"Audrey, please. Just do what he says," I say.

"Just because it doesn't matter how you look, Cindy doesn't mean I need to stop caring."

"Enough," Mom says, her words slow and lazy.

Canned laughter erupts from the television but none of us crack a smile. We missed the joke, but Sheldon is looking fairly smug over something.

"Why don't we put in Dawn of the Dead? Cindy has the DVD in her room," Audrey says, thinking she's being clever.

"Shut up," I hiss through my clenched teeth. My face feels hot. I'm not up for a lecture from Mom over what movies I shouldn't be watching. Unlike her, I can't hide behind a bottle of wine and pretend things are completely normal.

A barrage of commercials starts up, always much louder than the actual programs—McDonald's, Walmart, iPod. I'm not sure why they still play these stupid ads. Nobody is eating at McDonald's, and Walmart has sold out of nearly everything anyone might need during a zombie apocalypse. Unless you can stop zombies with cheap makeup or knock-off jewelry—they have plenty of those things left.

Finally, an overly-happy pop tune starts playing, overlaid with the vocals of a female who sounds like she's about twelve years old. "Don't you forget about me," she sings and I recognize the song from one of those 1980s teen flicks I watched with Mom last summer. A montage of children playing, a smiling mother, an active grandfatherly type, flickers across the screen.

"Remember, your loved ones retain their uniqueness, that thing made them "them" even after the transformation," a jovial announcer chimes in over the music. "At The Pastures, the transformation process is made easy for everyone. At The Pastures, you never have to say goodbye—until you're ready."

We all fall into a morbid, uncomfortable silence. Mom refills her glass. I glance at Audrey who shovels a heavy forkful of casserole into her blush mouth.

"The Pastures is the only long-term care facility of its kind in the area. Plus, some insurance plans are now being accepted. Just call 1-888-D-I-G-N-I-T-Y. The Pastures is safe for all concerned."

The squeaky-hipster chick vocals start up again.

I frown and look at Dad. He's thinking the same thing I am: "Do we *really* need a sales pitch?"

"That song reeks," Audrey says. "It's as lame as these dumb shows." Then she looks at me. "You going to finish that?" She nods toward my plate where a few bites of casserole remain.

"Go ahead." I shove the plate across the coffee table.

"Maybe I'll purge later," she whispers.

"You're a regular Lifetime movie," I say.

"Bitch," my sis counters.

"Dead bitch," I respond. That's one I'll regret. I know it.

CHAPTER 15

December 9
Cindy

I'm heading out to the car to wait for Audrey when the screaming starts. I just make it back into the main entrance of the school as the droves reach the front stairs.

Mr. Carlton and Mrs. Belle are waiting at the entrance.

A hoard of Shamblers swarm the parking lot just as school is being dismissed. Nobody knows where they came from or why there are so many, but they just keep coming—people of all ages, all colors. Children. The elderly. Most of them are dressed rather formally—the ladies in smart, modest dresses, the men in trousers, dress shirts, and ties. Like church clothes. Or funeral clothes.

But the one that will stick in my mind when I close my eyes tonight is the little boy. Dark-haired, sweet-faced, in a short-pants suit. His tie has come loose.

Blood stains his mouth like chocolate syrup and paints his tiny square teeth when he snarls.

A girl, whose name I never learned, is attacked as she gets into her car. An old man pulls her head back by the hair and tears into her throat, her shrill screaming dissolving into a wet gurgle. Her blonde hair goes rust-colored in a matter of seconds. Her ultra-cool hippie blouse changes to a hideous mess of splotchy red.

It's terrible to die that way.

She has a brand new leafy green Beetle. Her parents love her.

Love doesn't help anymore. My parents love me just like they love Audrey, but that's not enough.

In a moment, she's gone, vanished beneath a mass of writhing bodies.

These are our neighbors.

Those who are outside, flee to get back in. Some make it. There are others stuck inside their cars while the Shamblers pound stupidly on the windshield and the windows. Thank goodness their brain capacity has diminished so much that they no longer understand tools.

Melissa trips on the stairs, coming out of her silly high heels (who the hell wears heels to school during a zombie outbreak anyway?) and Mr. Carlton bursts through the doors. He snatches her up the stairs just before a girl of about six clamps down on her ankle with a set of decidedly Jack o' Lantern teeth.

"Get the door! Now!" he shouts, getting Melissa, and himself, through just in time.

Hands press the cool metal, and the thick glass and the heavy doors weigh nothing. Maybe a dozen of us shove those double doors closed, catching the little girl zombie halfway in.

Her head pops like an overripe melon (geez, what a cliche!).

Someone screams. Crying builds and echoes in the hallway.

"We killed her," Emma Sanford howls. She does some kind of weirdo dance around what's left of the kid.

I looked across to the other door. Nick stares back, his beautiful face strangely blank. Then his eyes touch mine for an electric moment.

He moves closer and whispers, "Why don't you come with me to the art room? We might be here for a while."

The art room is located in what is essentially the basement of the school. All of the fine art rooms are stuck in the dungeon. I guess that indicates what Palmdale High School thinks of creativity. The football team has a brand-new locker room and equipment. The levels of importance in the B.Z. (before zombies) years were jocks, academics, and then creatives. Of course, there were levels within those categories, too. For example, the varsity football team ruled over all jocks, with baseball players next, and basketball players after that (depending on which team enjoyed a better previous season). Golf, tennis, and then soccer, followed by track. And, of course, female athletics were behind all of those. The brains also ranked in this order—*mathetletes,* the science nerds, then literary geniuses. Creatives were all tossed into the "we pretend to be impressed, but you'll never get anywhere with that" category.

The art room is as silent as a tomb (bad comparison, but sue me), every little sound echoes. Nick flips on the overhead fluorescents and the room seems to warm a little. The oily-chemical smell of paint and the sharp, acrid stink of mineral spirits hangs heavy in the air.

"I'm thinking of quitting school until this is over," he says. "I don't think it matters now."

I don't know why, but this hits me like a punch in the stomach. It's bad enough not to see him outside of school, now that he and Audrey are through. But now he's going to stop coming to school, too?

"No, it doesn't," I say, making a pretty sad attempt at sounding nonchalant. "But don't you want to maintain some sense of normalcy?"

"Normalcy," Nick whispers, laughing. "You sound like you're in college already. Missing a few days while the world ends isn't going to hurt you."

I shrug, more flattered than I probably should be.

Nick goes over to the window. "We can see from here." He shoves a narrow table closer to the outside wall, just below the long set of high windows that line the side of the room. I let him help me up although I'm perfectly capable of climbing onto a table. His fingers trail across my ass and I pretend not to notice, then he leaps up next to me. The view is decent if looking at running feet is interesting.

Muffled cries, some intermittent screaming, groans and enraged grunting. Pounding and scratching on the front entrance doors, just above and to the left of where we are watching. It's a real symphony of horror, those sounds.

"I wonder how long we'll be here," Nick says.

"Maybe the police will come," I answer. "I just hope those things can't get inside."

"From what I've seen, they aren't any stronger than they were when they were alive. It's just when there's so many..."

"Like a swarm of bees," I say.

"Or a pack of wolves."

My phone buzzes inside my jacket pocket and I check it. A text from Audrey.

ur not dead, r u?

I reply: **n**

Audrey: **I am—almost. LOL.**

I close my eyes and sigh. It's not funny and she knows it.

"Audrey?" Nick asks.

"Yeah. I'll find her. It's not like she's leaving without me."

Nick smiles, hops off the table, and then puts out his hand to help me down. "I've stored some of my painting here," he tells me. "Want to see them?" He seems like he's about to share a secret, excited and shy at the same time.

"Sure."

I follow him to a far corner that's enclosed by tall shelves loaded with paints, markers, all sorts of papers, and art history books. Behind the wall of shelves are dozens of canvases of all sizes, leaning against the block wall. Nick sorts through them until he finds the ones he's looking for.

Finally, he picks up three small, square canvases. The first one is a portrait of a forty-something man, smiling. He's handsome behind a pair of wire-rimmed glasses. His hair is not quite neat and his tie is loose, but he looks genuinely happy. This could be a painting of Nick in twenty years, but he corrects me before I can say anything.

"My dad."

"You look alike."

"Yeah," Nick says. "He was always positive, you know? Up. He never looked at the dark side of things." He laughs. "If we got stuck on the side of the road with a flat tire, he'd make a game out of it. 'Look at that bird, Nicky.' or 'I wonder if we change this thing faster than pit crew.' It was dumb sometimes…"

"That's not a dumb way to be, Nick." I sigh, thinking of the bleakness we now live in. The only positive is living through another day.

"Well. Either way, I find myself wondering if Dad might've been the lucky one. He never had to see this..."

"Don't think like that," I say. That was dumb—what am I going to back that up with? Don't think like that—we'll all be fine tomorrow?

Nick looks at me like he wants to hear reassurance that I cannot offer. He places the paintings back into the corner without offering to show the other two.

I start to say something else, suddenly the snap of gunfire echoes from out front of the school, making both of us jump.

"Shit," Nick says. "The cops are here."

"It's about time," I respond, although I'm in no particular hurry to leave.

He jumps back up onto the long table to get a better look out the window and turns, his hand outstretched. "Coming?"

"I don't need to see."

A man's voice blasts through a bullhorn, mechanical and lifeless. **"STAY INSIDE THE SCHOOL UNTIL THIS AREA IS CONTAINED. ANYONE LEAVING THE BUILDING WILL BE SHOT."**

Nick cups his hands around his face to cut the glare from the window and I take him in—his shaggy hair and his perfect body in those jeans—his back pocket is ripped and hanging halfway off. He's beautiful. Too beautiful to die a raving monster.

Of course, so is Audrey.

And in that case, so am I. And grandma, Mr. Carlton, the little boy we saw at the mall, and everyone else in Palmdale.

I used to think we were untouchable, but we're just like everyone else. Always breathing what might be our last breaths.

"Oh my God," Nick whispers, his voice shaky with horror.

"What?" I'm almost afraid to hear his answer.

"I think they're shooting everyone."

"What do you mean?" My throat wants to close up.

"They're shooting kids, Cindy. Kids who aren't even sick. And teachers. They're not stopping to check. They're killing everyone who's outside! They were serious."

I'm about to call Audrey when she crashes through the door to the art room.

"Bitch! I've been looking for you everywhere!"

Later, as Audrey drives home, I can't help noticing how her face isn't exactly the right color anymore. Her skin flakes around the cheeks and the chin. Audrey was always the last person to have skin issues. Plus, she smells a little ... funky, like gym shorts left in a locker too long. The medicine isn't working. Dad's used all of our money on a piece of shit vaccine that isn't going to save Audrey, or any of us, in the end.

I don't say anything about it, and she doesn't ask me why I was hanging out alone with Nick. Fair enough.

"You know, when the National Guard showed up this afternoon, they shot Chloe Marshall in the back of the head. She wasn't even infected. Only too stupid to get back inside."

She turns on the radio. Nothing but news, static, news, and that scary-weird emergency signal. I look out the window and watch the community I once loved pass me by.

December 11
Cindy

Audrey weeps like her heart's splitting in two, and I cannot sleep because it comes through the walls like water through a sponge. My sister, the tough one of us. The badass. The one who doesn't give a shit. She's dying and she knows she's dying. Does she wonder what's on the other side?

I know she's afraid. Why can't she just admit it?

I climb out of bed, the floor cold under my feet. Do Dad and Mom not hear her, or do they pretend not to, just like they pretended not to smell pot on her clothes, or notice her coming home an hour after curfew? Noticing doesn't make them bad parents, I want to tell them sometimes. It just made them parents.

I rap on her door, timid because she's always blown up if I enter her room without asking.

"Audrey? You okay?"

There's this small whimper—something that couldn't possibly come from my sister.

I open the door and pad into her room. Has she changed more? Will she leap on me and rip out my throat?

The smell is rotten, and cloying. My eyes water and the darkness becomes runny in front of my eyes.

"Audrey?" I whisper again.

"I wish I had longer," a small voice says from the shadows of the bed covers.

I cannot see her.

"I'm so cold," she says.

I climb into the bed next to her, afraid of her, yet afraid of what it'll be like without her. She's part of me. When she goes, it'll prove I'm nothing special. I can go at any moment, as well.

I snuggle against my sister's back, her body icy through Dad's silly oversized college t-shirt.

I stroke her hair and try not to notice how brittle it's become.

"I'm not ready to turn," Audrey says, her words drowning against her pillow.

"I'm not ready for you to turn," I say. "You gotta hang on. We'll get through this. Keep taking the shots and keep fighting."

"Tired of fighting," she whispers.

I have nothing else to say. We lie there, silent for a while. Finally, I notice her breathing has become heavy and deep, and I leave her alone. When I get back to my own bed, I cannot sleep for the rest of the night.

CHAPTER 16

🌢

December 18
Cindy

Seeing Audrey looking like she does makes me sick to my stomach and my heart. Since the end of school Friday, things have gotten much worse. She's sick and still trying to hide it. Dad's still jabbing her full of Phalanx, but I know he can see it's not working. Still, like Mom, he's pretending we're all going to live happily ever after.

Half the time, I just want to puke.

Aside from seeing Nick in the hallway, my only other bright spot is Mr. Carlton's class. But even he's lost something—the thing that made me squirm in my seat the first part of the school year. His "spark," as Mom calls it. He hasn't shaved in at least three days and bruises have set in beneath his eyes.

"Why do you think we're still coming to school?" he asks once the few of us who are still bothering to show up get settled.

There's a long, uncomfortable silence. Nobody wants to answer—saying it makes it real, just like I've said before. But finally, I answer because Mr. Carlton looks so used up that I don't want him to have to say it.

"It's because we are all living in denial, Mr. Carlton."

"Okay, Cindy. I think you're right. But why?"

I bite my lip, trying to think of the right words, but from the back, Darius Williams beat me to it. "Because it's a defense mechanism. If we don't tell ourselves everything is going to be fine, we're all going to go crazy."

"What's left of us, you mean," Bree Anders whispers.

"My mom says it's part of the five stages of dying," Darius continues. His mother is the psychologist at Palmdale Middle. "Denial, anger, bargaining, depression and acceptance."

Mr. Carlton nods. "I think you guys are right. Do you think we are coping with the N-Virus as a society as a whole or separately?"

"I believe each person deals with it differently," I offer. "I mean some families haven't been hit as hard as others. Most of us are still in denial, just like Darius said."

"Exactly," Darius agrees. "And there are others who have lost nearly everything. Those people are probably experiencing anger."

"Just say it, D-Dog. They're damned pissed," Cole Jagger chimes in from the seat just behind me. "My dad's sick, and wandering around in The Pastures like one of the Walking Dead, and that makes me pissed."

I turn and glance at him. I don't think any of us knew. He's always been a quiet tough guy, a little more mature than the rest of us.

"I'm sorry," I whisper, knowing it does nothing to help. If my dad was in The Pastures, I'm pretty sure I wouldn't be sitting in this stupid, nearly empty classroom.

Cole nods. "Thanks. It's not like I'm the only one, but still…"

Does he mean Audrey?

"Either way, I've decided this is a free day," Mr. Carlton says. "You can do what you want to. Choose to read whatever you want, take out your iPads, and watch a movie. Or we can just talk for an hour."

Avery Adams says, "I'm going to watch Dawn of the Dead on Netflix. We can learn more from that than we can from Shakespeare." He's such a horror and sci-fi geek, I just assumed he already knew what to do in the event of a zombie uprising.

There's a rumble of hardy agreement. I spend most of the hour looking out the window, to the empty courtyard. It's drizzling, cold, and overall pretty shitty outside, but better than trying to read something that doesn't matter or talk about things that we can't control. Or worse, talk about stupid things that no longer matter.

At the end of the class, Mr. Carlton hands out a week's worth of reading and discussion assignments. "I don't know why you continue to come here—it's dangerous. Shit, (I've never heard a teacher swear before, but extraordinary circumstances and all that...) you people blow off school for snow flurries around here, but show up during the zombie apocalypse. We'll meet on Skype on Tuesdays and Thursdays. 1:00. I assume everyone can get Skype, correct?"

There's a murmur of agreement.

"The numbers and information are on the assignment packet."

"Can I be naked?" someone from the back of the room asks. A male voice—typical.

"Try to be fully clothed," Mr. Carlson answers, "at least from the waist up.

Things hit the fan out in the hallway just after lit class, when Audrey sort of lumbers passed, looking more than a little out of it—she's especially tired today, she mentioned in the car on the way to school. She insisted on driving, but I think it's not such a great idea to ride with an almost zombie. I don't mean to sound cold, but sometimes, I feel that being cold is the only way a person can adapt and survive this.

She doesn't say anything, which is not like her. Audrey is the center of attention, no matter whether she's in the hall, the class, the mall, or on the sidelines. As I mentioned, her bitch-posses are down to only two, and those two seem to be backups—clone cheerleaders who were cast to understudy roles from the beginning, and eager for an opening in the main, bird-brained clique.

"Look at her. She's turning into one of them, and yet she's still here." Tommy says when she's just out of earshot. Still, it's loud enough for everyone else to hear,

Everyone else includes Nick, who pushes me aside before I can stop him, and maybe I wasn't going to stop him, anyway. Before I know it, he and Tommy are on the floor rolling around like maniacs, fists flying, sneakers kicking up.

The crowd tightens around and I push forward. Nick is straddling Tommy's chest, but I need to stop him before he gets hurt—Tommy outweighs him by at least twenty pounds, so in a moment, the momentum will change. I'm just amazed Tommy's asshole clone entourage (similar to Audrey's bitch-posse) hasn't tried to intervene. Funny how a little thing like an epidemic changes peoples' behavior.

"Don't, Nick. He's not worth this. He's not worth anything!" I shout.

I tug at his arm, but he shrugs me away. I could've been a baby, for all I was doing to stop him. His fist connects with Tommy's mouth, and blood comes slow and thick.

"Stop it now, you two idiots!" Mr. Carlton snatches Nick off of Tommy and then pulls Tommy to his feet by the front of his shirt.

"Look at you!" he snarls, planting himself between them. "You have no idea how stupid this is."

"You as good as killed her, you shit!" Nick says, glaring at Tommy.

Tommy lunges at Nick, but Mr. Carlton shoves him back, although he barely comes up to Tommy's chin. "Enough." He turns to Nick. "Both of you."

Tommy smiles, revealing a mouthful of bloody teeth, and the little hairs on my arms prickle. For a moment, he looks just like he's infected. I shiver and then touch Nick's shoulder. "It doesn't matter, Nick. Not anymore."

Nick turns to me, the rage still evident on his face. "But it does..."

"No. It doesn't," I whisper, taking his hand. I lead him away from the stupid, staring Palmdale High School leftovers.

Ten minutes later, I realized I'd left my phone on my desk in Mr. Carlton's classroom. I never do that—forget things, but my mind's been going in circles since we learned we're no longer required to show up for class. Another nail in the coffin of normalcy, I suppose.

The shit's gettin' real. Someone said that once, trying to be funny. Looking back, it's not funny at all. Besides, the shit's been real for months. It was real the day that the first infected rolled into the E.R., whether we wanted to believe it or not.

Mr. Carlton is bent over his desk with his face in his hands. He jerks his head up, startled when I enter, and drags his palms across his eyes.

"I'm...I'm sorry, Mr. Carlson. I forgot my phone." I feel awkward, having caught him crying like that.

"No. It's fine, Cindy."

I hurry to my desk and snatch up the phone, dropping and spilling my bag in the process. "Shit," I mutter, bending to scoop up everything. Then I add, "Sorry," my face growing hot. What the hell? At the end of the world, I'm going to worry about swearing in front of my teacher.

He's watching me, his face weary, making me feel even more self-conscious.

"Okay," I say, forcing a smile. I hurry back toward the door, wanting to get out of there. Never have I wanted to get away from Mr. Carlton? Before the N-Virus, I was sad when his class was over every day.

But I stop and turn back to him. "Mr. Carlton, are you okay?" Yeah, that was a stupid thing to ask—people who're caught crying typically aren't okay.

"I—uh—no," he stammers. Then after a moment he says, "My fiancé contracted the N-Virus. She turned six days ago."

"Oh. Oh, sh— I'm so sorry." I move closer to him, unsure what to do. I touch his shoulder and feel bone there. I never guessed he was so thin.

"She came after me. I got home from school, she was there. Bitten, throat gone. Blood everywhere." He shakes, fighting to hold back fresh tears, and he again covers his face with his hands. "She jumped on me, growling low like some monster from a dumb horror movie, and knocked me to the floor, pinning me down. She screamed into my face, but the sound was airy like a whisper because most of her throat was gone. Her teeth snapped at my face, her eyes..." He sighs and slides his hands down his face, then stares at me like he's reliving every moment by telling me.

"Don't, Mr. Carlson."

"Let me. I think I need to." He takes hold of my wrist, begging me to stay until his story is told. But I don't want to stay because I know where it's going. It's going to the same place Audrey's story is.

"I squirmed out from under her, and she clutched at my shirt, ripping it, but I managed to climb to my feet."

The words pour from him like a flood. I doubt he can stop, even if he wanted to. I stand there, his warm, damp hand on my wrist, wanting to bolt from the nightmare he's creating inside my mind.

"I grab the fireplace shovel from the hearth, a gift from her aunt and uncle when we bought our house, and I hit her with it." His voice drops low as if he believes someone else is also listening.

"I hit her again and again, but she keeps coming, keeps screaming that horrible, airy scream."

"You didn't do anything wrong, Mr. Carlton." I stroke his shoulder again. I've never been any good at comforting. A wannabe doctor with shitty bedside manners, that's me. It probably wouldn't have worked out, after all.

"Finally she went down and stayed and I got the hell out of there. I grabbed what I could—a few photos, my iMac, and haven't been back."

"I'm really sorry," I say again. What else is there to say? I am sorry. I'm sorry for myself, mostly, but I'm just like everyone else.

"Maybe that should be the theme for this year's prom," he laughs. "No going back."

I force myself to laugh with him, yet unable to find any humor in it at all. "I think you're right," I agree.

Mr. Carlton stands up and for an instant, I flash on one of the many girly-crush scenarios that played in my mind over the past school year. He puts his arms around me, but none of the feelings I'd imagined in my fantasies show up.

"Take care of yourself, Cindy," he says, his breath soft against the side of my neck.

"I will." I draw away. "Skype on Thursday?"

He nods and I leave the classroom knowing I'll never see Mr. Carlton again.

CHAPTER 17

●

December 21
Cindy

Sure, I'd love to have a Tom Holland kind of guy show up and save the day—and he can be in those Spiderman tights if he wants. At first, seeing the illness spread was like watching a weed grow, but weeds get out of control and take over the healthy grass. Before very long, there's nothing left but the weeds. Everything else is dead or dying.

Sometimes, I look out my bedroom window and wonder what things will be like in a year. Tonight, I notice the house across the street—the Harrellsons—empty and looks like it has been for a few weeks. The Harrellsons were one of those picture-perfect families, a mom, and dad, in their early thirties, with big, capped smiles, and two cherub-faced babies, a boy and a girl, both under the age of three. All four with hair as yellow as the sun and a wardrobe of bright Lilly Pulitzer and Lacoste. They were young, perfect, and a bit sickening, frankly.

Still, I hate to see their house abandoned. There's an ill feeling in the pit of my belly, wondering which of them became infected. Perhaps all of them, and now they are dead or nearly dead, and wandering around The Pastures with their expensive clothing and expressionless eyes. How they loved those children.

Imagining small children, barely walking, white-eyed Shamblers is nearly too much, even after everything I've seen.

There should be a festive wreath hanging on their front door.

Through the bedroom wall, Audrey is screaming, her voice like she's swallowed broken glass. I push my earbuds into my ears, but I don't turn on the music. I crave silence, but cannot find it, because I hear my heart beating in my ears like a dull bass.

Dad brought out the big, artificial Christmas tree from the attic. We hadn't used it since Audrey and I were small, always choosing to buy a fresh tree instead. I hate that Christmas is like this, I hate that nobody cares about it. It doesn't matter if they are religious or not. It's a holiday about family, and every family I know right now is broken. Or at least splintered.

I miss the piney scent of last year's Christmas tree. Now it seems like everything has the stink of rot around it. I go outside and it's there, hanging in the cool air. I stay inside and I can smell Audrey...decaying...and she's not even dead yet.

Nick gave me an early Christmas gift. It was a painting of a bold-looking Cindy Scott riding a silver dragon. It's quite lovely, but it's not me. Not by a long shot. I gave him a jump drive full of music—indie stuff, vapid 80s music, and even some "hippie" music, as he calls it. I hadn't expected him to give me anything, and I backed up that collection of music before I gave it to him.

It's not like I was able to make a trip over to the mall for holiday shopping this year, you know.

Peace, love, and all that shit. Those same peace freaks are the ones beating the hell out of each other for a gallon of gasoline or a carton of eggs.

People really suck, it turns out. Living and dead, they all kinda suck.

January 3
Cindy

Christmas came and went, and so did New Year's, but we decided to not bother. Maybe it's morbid, but Dad's too tired from his shifts at the hospital, Mom's too drunk, and it's just too hard to make myself smile when I'd rather scream.

It's been two weeks since we stopped attending school, but maybe that's okay. Audrey isn't in the physical or mental state to continue on. I would've felt like an asshole going without her.

If you've ever had someone you love who is dying of a terminal illness, you know it doesn't matter how much you love them. At some point, when things get really ugly—for them and for you—you realize you're just ready for it to be over.

What you loved was the "normal" them anyway. Not the diseased them. That's what's happened with Audrey.

I hate that I feel this way, but I can't stop it.

Anyway, Audrey is becoming one of the—a Shambler—and the longer she sticks around like this, the tougher it is to remember how she was before. Sure, she was a bitch sometimes or maybe even most times, but I loved her. I still love her.

I don't know what to think now. She's failing quickly. Mom and Dad go to her, but Mom's afraid of her and Dad just goes in to shove the needle into her arm. That vaccine does nothing more than drain our finances. Audrey's college funds are gone and mine are almost gone.

She screams and thrashes against the wall. I worked up the nerve to go into her room a few days ago—I'd not seen her in about three days. She was sitting on the floor, wearing only one of Dad's oversized t-shirts, rocking back and forth.

Her hair hung in greasy, bloody strands, covering her face. She was holding a tube of bright lipstick—a shade of pink that looked good in summer when Audrey was tanned and perfect. She'd smeared it all over her mouth and up on her cheeks, a weird girly version of Batman's Joker.

Worse than that, blood and what may be shit, judging from the odor, had been wiped all over one wall like some kind of disgusting mural.

"Audrey?" I whispered. "Do you need anything?" My voice shook, fighting the urge to retch.

"Hungry," she rasped. "So fucking hungry, but none of you give a shit."

I opened my mouth to respond, but there was nothing to say. I back out of her room and close the door behind me.

CHAPTER 18

🝡

January 5
Cindy

It was one of those screwy dreams that only come when you're first drifting off. In it, I think I'm juggling a soccer ball, knee to knee, instep, instep, again and again. It's so easy in my dream world like there's no gravity and the ball is filled with helium. I laugh at my incredible new skill (I'd never been an expert at juggling), the sound of the ball striking my knees—a dull *twack, twack, twack.*

But the sound gets louder, faster, and no longer in time with the motion of the ball.

"Cindy. Cindy. Open up," a voice enters the dream. Nick.

I jump awake, acutely aware that I was asleep and dreaming. It's Saturday evening. The sky is just becoming dark, but sleep has been so fleeting lately. Audrey rants incoherently at the top of her lungs and wakes me up a couple of times a night.

"Cindy."

I glance at the window, bleary-eyed and confused. A pale face stares back. I gasp, my heart lurching, because it's only

Nick. His breath fogs the glass, and he smears it away with his fist.

I unlatch the window and push it up, a rush of cold air touches my face. "What the hell? You scared me to death."

"Sorry."

I stand there, awkward and unsure of what to say for a moment. Finally, Nick asks, "Did I wake you?"

"Yeah, but it's no big deal."

Nick laughs. "I guess we all have."

"Why are you up here?" I ask.

"I tried the door, but nobody answered. I didn't think you all were out at the mall."

"No. Dad's probably at the hospital. He's been staying there a few nights a week. Mom must be asleep." Or passed out.

Nick pulls a bottle from the inside of his ski jacket and holds it up, rather proudly. "Come out here."

"Isn't it cold?" I ask, but I grab the blanket from my bed and climb out onto the roof.

"You'll be warm soon enough," Nick tells me, but I know he means from the liquor. Too bad.

I'd never been out there, on the roof, because I'm afraid of heights, but the slope is slight and it's not too bad. The moon is fat and silvery, and cold sharpens my drowsy mind quickly. It feels as though I haven't been out in days, and I suppose I haven't. Dad and Mom have decided that it's too dangerous to get out and run. The treadmill is a royal drag, but it's better than nothing. Besides, it's only for a short while.

I'm still telling myself that. But it's becoming more difficult to buy into it.

We sit there staring at the nearly deserted neighborhood, huddled close under the blanket, and quickly I'm warm all over except my toes. Last year at this time, the Christmas lights would've still been twinkling in the clear night in the waning glow of the holidays.

But this isn't like last year. The houses are dark and the little fancy-assed English-style street lamps that line the street seem too dim, creating heavy shadows that are prime hangout spots for Shamblers and other dangerous assholes.

"You know it's dangerous out here, don't you?" I say.

"I was careful." He looks straight up at the sky. "Cops are as bad as the Shamblers. Cruising around, ready to hassle anyone who's out."

"Well, you're not supposed to be out. You could get bitten. Or killed." I want to scold him, but the fact is I'm glad he's here. "Or arrested."

"I'm not sure which would be worse."

"Me neither," I agree.

He twists the top from the bottle and takes a drink. "Here." He offers it to me.

"What the hell is it?" I ask, holding the bottle up toward the scant light. "Vanilla-flavored Rum?" I smell it first—not bad, but overly sweet. I take a cautious drink, expecting the harsh burn that comes with whiskey. Not that I drink a lot of whiskey, but I have tasted it a couple of times. Nasty.

This stuff was nothing like that. I take another, longer swig before passing it back to Nick.

"Careful," he tells me, laughing. "It's sneaky." He takes another drink. "You know, I heard the military has been rounding people up. Not just the carriers, either, but well people," Nick says. "I've heard that they're killing people. Just like at the school, but more."

I shake my head. "That can't be true. At least I hope not." Another drink. It's going down a lot easier now.

"I think it is. I overheard Miles on his cell. They say it's the only way to contain the virus. Killing everyone who might've been in contact with the carriers."

I open my mouth to say something, but Audrey starts up her screaming again. The dull thrashing sound of her pounding, and throwing herself against the wall thumps like a broken drum.

"Shit," Nick half-hisses, half-whispers. "Is that—"

I cut him off. "Yeah."

He sits upright and presses his face against his knees. He folds his hands over the back of his head like he's trying to stop blocking out the sound. "I can't believe things are like this." His words are muffled against the fabric of his jeans. "My grandma. Audrey. It's just so shitty."

I stroke his back, feeling his back moving with his breath. "I can't either. It's like a nightmare that I can't wake from."

We drink in companionable silence while Audrey finishes up her screaming fit. This one doesn't last as long as usual, and I'm relieved. She's not here any longer—there's only this angry, hungry thing living inside her room, living inside her rotting flesh. I wish it was all over.

"I was going nuts at home," Nick says. "I never really liked school. It was boring and most of the kids were jerks. But now...it's like there's nothing. At least school was something. You know? Mom cries a lot. Miles claims he's working double shifts, but I suspect he's only patrolling because it gives him a chance to act like a dick without suffering the consequences. (Little sister) pretends Grandma will get better and we'll just go pick her up from the Pastures like nothing ever happened.

"Yeah. I know." I laugh. "I actually miss some of those jerks. Even dumbass Jake Wylie."

"Really?" Nick asks, his eyebrows raising.

"Well, no. Not really." I giggle. The rum is taking hold. My head is swims pleasantly and things don't seem as dire as they had an hour ago.

Nick laughs despite the tears shining around his eyes. "Yeah, you do. We all do. Even those annoying asshats are better than this." He nods toward the empty street.

The lights flicker on and a halo of mist shimmers around each one. The houses are so quiet, so empty. Sawgrass Flats is half populated now if that.

"Do you worry about it?"

Nick turns to me, frowning. "What 'it?' I worry about everything now. My family. Well, not Miles because he's a dick, but Mom and Micah. I worry that things will never be the same, I'll never go to college, never marry, never do the things a normal guy should do."

"That's what I mean. Never having the chance to do the things you want to do."

Nick tilts his face upward toward the clouding evening sky.

"I guess there's no more waiting for the right moment," he whispers. "Those moments are too fleeting."

"You're right." I reach over and place my hand on top of his. Despite the fact that my heart feels like it's going to jump right through my chest, I feel bold suddenly. He doesn't pull away.

"Don't get mad, Nick," I say. Then I do it. I lean close, and I kiss him.

His mouth is cool, soft. At first he doesn't react, and I immediately wish I hadn't done anything. "Sorry."

"Don't be," he says. "I was just...surprised." He takes my face in his hands and kisses me, and his lips are warmer, his tongue pressing against my tongue.

Behind us, Audrey grunts, and slaps the windows with her open hands. Does she know what's happening? Does she even remember who Nick is (was)? I break the kiss and stand, my balance is iffy because of the drinking. Nick jumps to his feet and grabs my shoulders, steadying me.

"Told you the rum was a sneaky bastard."

I take his hand and lead him through my bedroom window. Audrey's growls and cries grow slightly more muffled, but I can still hear her. I dock my iPod, hit shuffle, and Velvet Underground's "Sweet Jane" fills the room, melancholy and hopeful at the same time.

"Old stuff?" Nick says. "Are you sure you and Audrey are from the same parents?"

I don't have a reply because anything I say about her now is pretty shitty. She's turning into a walking corpse and I just kissed her boyfriend. Well, ex-boyfriend. We lie back across the bed, taking turns with the rum again listening to the music, listening to Audrey's fit in the next room. I know what I should feel, and what I do feel. The two aren't even close, and I take Nick's face in my hands and kiss him again.

He responds with his mouth and his cool hands, and the press of his body against mine. My mind swirls with the drink, and I wonder if I am having an incredibly vivid dream.

I've never gone further than kissing with a boy. Nick has his hands under my shirt, sliding over my bra, lacing his fingers under my bra. I tense and he must sense it.

"Sorry," he tells me, and his hands are gone.

"Why?" I ask. "Tomorrow we might be dead. We might be like Audrey and the rest of them."

"No. Don't say that, Cindy." He props up on his elbow and looks down at me, his perfect face half in shadow. He pushes my hair from my face and smiles. "We're not like the rest of them. Don't forget that. Do you hear me?"

He leans close and kisses my nose. "We're drunk."

I smile. "So?"

"So, I should get home."

Nick kisses me again, the way a guy who has no plans of leaving might kiss. But in a moment, he's gone, vanished through the window and into the unpredictable suburban night.

January 18
Cindy

It's around 10 o'clock when something flashes past my bedroom door. Knowing Mom's been "asleep" for hours, and

Dad is likely at the hospital under the guise of helping people, something in the pit of my stomach does a funky flip-flop when I realize who (or what) it is.

I put aside the sketch pad half-full of drawings that Nick gave me the other night, but I keep the pencil in my fist as I slip out into the dark hallway.

"Audrey?" I half-whisper, which is stupid since Mom's not waking for anything (except maybe another glass of wine), and Audrey isn't answering. I flip on the light. I haven't seen Audrey for nearly a week. Dad places sedatives in her raw ground meat—beef, turkey, pork—whatever we can get our hands on—and slips it into the door quickly like he's feeding a raging lion. Once he knows she's out, he enters her room and jabs the useless Phalanx into her vein like he can't see what she's become.

There's a slug's trail of black-red blood and ooze on the hallway floor and along the walls here and there. It stinks of decayed meat, and I would puke if I'd eaten anything tonight. With Mom in her state, and Dad staying away as much as he does, I get away with not eating most nights. The muscle tone in my legs has diminished, and my clothes are looser, but nothing major. Yet.

Something in my brain tells me to go as light as I can stand on what little food we have left. Besides, I can't eat when I'm scared, and I'm scared nearly all the fucking time lately.

Just like now.

My hands shake, and I call Audrey again. The pencil is sweating in my fist.

Then I hear her moaning. Not those fake zombie-groans like on The Walking Dead. It's more of a mournful weeping sound if wild animals could weep. That's the sound I've learned comes from the Shamblers—that sad moaning and screaming. Enraged, frustrated, starved screaming.

I've become used to both coming through the walls of Audrey's bedroom.

There's a dull thumping noise, and I realize she's stumbling down the stairs. Part of me wants her to get outside. That would take the weight of taking care of her off my back. A cop or a soldier would take her out and this would all be over.

At least Audrey's chapter would be finished.

I jog down the stairs, careful not to kill myself on the slick mess my sister's leaving behind on the floor, and see her crooked, spidery shape silhouetted against the wintery moon glow pouring through the kitchen windows. At first, I can't tell whether she is facing me or looking outside.

"Come on, sis. Let's get you back upstairs."

She groans softly and turns toward my voice. Her face is hidden behind a thick, tangled veil of dark hair.

"Audrey?"

Her head jerks again and again as if there's a broken hinge in her neck. In the quiet of the house, there's the faint splatting sound of blood or waste leaving her body. Her odor is rancid enough to make my eyes water, and I try to breathe through my mouth—something I'm growing more accustomed to.

Then for a few moments, Audrey becomes perfectly still. The jerking stops. The groaning stops. There's only that dripping sound.

My mouth is so dry, and my heart is pounding like something is going wrong with my body.

I open my mouth to speak to her again, but she suddenly drops her head back, turning her face to the ceiling.

She shrieks.

The shrillness of her voice is inhuman, like a siren blaring directly into my ears.

I drop the pencil and do not have enough wits to grab a kitchen knife or any other thing to defend myself. As she takes a clumsy step toward me, I thrust a kitchen chair toward her, making her stumble, and tear out of the kitchen and into Dad's office.

The gun is in his desk drawer and the thought flashes through my mind. I can't allow my face to be ripped off, but still, she's my sister. I leave the gun alone and crawl under the desk, pulling Dad's heavy leather chair in behind me.

Shamblers aren't smart, and they aren't quick. She may never realize where I am. I just pray Mom doesn't stagger down for a glass of water, or Dad doesn't walk into the house and into Audrey's hunger-crazed arms.

I pull my knees up and press my face against the soft flannel of my pajamas, fighting the need to cry, and biting back the scream that's building in my throat.

How the hell did she get out? Did Mom leave her room unlocked? Maybe she has a reason that's only evident to people who are drunk and hopeless.

Either way, blaming Mom isn't helping me right now. Something crashes and shatters on the floor. The funk of Audrey's decaying body grows stronger.

I bite my bottom lips, drawing a thin taste of blood, and try to make myself even smaller under the desk. Audrey screams, and the sound is like she's swallowed broken glass. How has Mom not heard this?

She's at the desk now—I can make out the shape of her body against the scant light coming in around the windows. She's become the color of ash, dressed in panties and one of Dad's Blue Devil t-shirts. Her icy toes brush my toes as she pushes toward the desk, stupid and unaware of the chair that's between us. I yank my foot away, biting back a cry. I never imagined how cold she'd become.

I've heard they can smell the living. I know I can sure as hell smell the dead.

A wheezing sigh and she then tugs at the chair. Maybe she's not so stupid after all. But I grip it with everything I have to stop her from pulling it away, exposing my safe spot.

She tugs at the chair once again and this time, she almost snatches it from my grasp. Screaming, she begins shoving it hard back toward the desk. Frustrated and angry, she sounds like a wild thing. I can't say animal because no living animal has ever sounded that way.

"No! Audrey?" Mom's there. God, I hope she's not too close.

A door slams. More hard thumps and shuffling, followed by a breath of silence.

Suddenly, I'm staring into the dead eyes of my older sister as she tastes the floor.

Weeks ago Dad learned it was best to keep a super-octane sedative in one pocket of his lab coat. In the other pocket, he carries a 9mm in the other. I don't know where he got it and I don't care. I'm afraid to think of how many times he has used it lately. Saving people and killing them at the same time, I suppose.

But it was the sedative he used on Audrey because that's the only way a dad can react.

"Cindy?" Dad calls.

"I'm under the desk."

He removes the chair and takes my hand and I notice we're both trembling. I can hear Mom weeping somewhere in the corner, still hidden in the shadows. I fall against his chest, suddenly woozy and exhausted.

"Meg," Dad says. "Get these lights on. That sedative will wear off soon enough. We need to get Audrey back up to her room."

Back in my bed, I can't fall asleep. I'm still too jacked up over almost dying only an hour ago. I press my head against the wall, doing what I know I shouldn't be.

"What the hell happened, Meg?" Dad's never raised his voice to any of us. Even now, his voice is even, his anger contained.

"I don't know. I took her a little food and peeked in at her for a while. I guess I forgot to lock it back. I just forgot, Ben."

"Well, you'd better get it together. Our other daughter was nearly killed tonight because you cannot go an hour without a drink lately."

"But everything's fine, now. We'll get another lock. A better one."

"What good does any kind of lock do, if you leave it unlocked?" He sighs. "We've done all we could. It's time to make the call."

"What do you mean?" Mom sobs.

"I mean Audrey is gone. We need to allow her some dignity. We can't keep her here like she is.

"Although I'd prefer to just put her down, I'll call The Pastures in the morning."

Mom mutters some response, but I cannot make it out. I've heard all I needed to hear, anyway.

I pull away from the wall, press my face against my pillow, and wonder why I cannot find any more tears for my sister.

CHAPTER 19

🜄

January 21
Cindy

"Call 1-888-Dignity," it says on the side of the van, just like Nick had mentioned. It's a harsh-looking prisoner transport wrapped with too-bright images of rolling hills and big live oak. So tranquil that you almost forget your family member has become a raging zombie.

The undertaker for The Pastures refers to himself as a "transition director." His name is Melvin Erwin ("just call me Mel"), and he's packing heat under his black jacket. Dad makes all the arrangements as Mom sits silently, dry-eyed, and out of it. Dad has given her Valium. That scares me a little since she can't stay out of the wine.

Mel goes over some different packages, all of which are somewhat costly as compared to just putting the infected person down if you ask me. I don't mean to sound heartless, just realistic. Dead is dead, and the ability to walk and eat doesn't make them any less dead. Mel also goes over memorial services, suggesting the home service, considering the dangers of being "out and about at the moment."

"Thank you, but no. We'll have a private remembrance here. There's no need for anything more. There's so much death. Funerals have become pointless," Dad tells him. "Just see to our daughter. Make her as comfortable as possible."

When they wrap things up, Mel takes out his cell. "We're ready," he says, then puts the phone back into the breast pocket of his jacket. In seconds, four heavily-armed, heavily-armored, muscle-bound dudes in baseball caps with "The Pastures" logo appears at the front door, ready to escort Audrey to her new home.

Apparently, they are extremely efficient with what they do. Within ten minutes, Audrey emerges down the stairs, strapped to a hospital gurney, dressed in the dark purple frock she loathed but kept because Grandma bought it for her. What irony—Audrey set for the rest of her days in an outfit she hates. She's barefoot because even the best "transition director" can't keep shoes on the living dead. Her hair is a mad tangle, and her eyes are as pale as her flesh, staring upward at the ceiling. Her lips have been completely chewed away. She smells so bad that I want to get out of there, but I force myself to stay. She's shackled at the wrists and ankles, despite being belted to the gurney. She's been dosed with some sort of tranquilizer, I assume, as she's quiet and barely moving.

Mom approaches, wearing a loopy, somewhat inappropriate smile, as the men move toward the front door. "Can I say goodbye to her?"

"Yes, Ma'am," Mel answers, "but I must request that you do not touch her."

"But she's strapped down. She's handcuffed," Mom argues.

"Meg. Please—" Dad begins. He places his hands on her shoulders, but she shrugs them away.

"It's for your own safety, Mrs. Scott. I realize how difficult this must be, but the tranquilizers have only limited effect on those in this stage of infection. And every case is different. She may wake at any moment."

Mom gives Mel a look like she'd be just as happy to see his head explode.

"Meg. Say goodbye," Dad whispers.

I move closer and take Mom's hand, but Mom pulls away from me just as she did Dad. Maybe this should've hurt my feelings, but it doesn't. Audrey was always her favorite, anyway. I came to terms with that sometime around my tenth birthday when Audrey told me that Mom had shared that little tidbit with her when they we out shopping together.

Mom then leans close to Audrey and says something I can't make out, then heads upstairs without another word.

I can't think of anything profound to say, so "See ya on the other side, Big Sis" pops out of my mouth. My face grows hot even though there's nobody there for me to feel embarrassed in front of. I then head to the kitchen, leaving Dad to say his goodbyes.

The house becomes like a tomb once Audrey is gone. Not hearing her screams isn't any better than hearing them. I listen to music and try to sketch, but my mind's everywhere, and nothing I think of is positive. I text Nick about what's happened, and he responds with a sad face followed in a few minutes with **"OK if I come ovr ltr?"**

I need him more than he realizes, and more than I can express to him just yet. Sure, society is falling all around us, but I don't want to come across as needy.

Dad gave Mom another Valium, and she's sleeping in her black go-to-funerals-and-fancy-party dress, sprawled across her bed, uncovered, still wearing her shiny black pumps. Her normally perfect makeup is smudged, making the little lines around her eyes stand out. She looks old. Old and worn out.

After a moment, I decide to crawl onto the bed next to her, feeling a little strange because we'd never been that close—it was always Mom and Audrey on one side and Dad and me on the other. I reach out and take her bony, cool hand in mine. I don't think I've held her hand since I was ten, and feel bad for not being a better daughter. She hasn't been able to speak to Grandma in weeks, but she's hanging in there. We can't help but think the worse, so, I'll hand it to her. Maybe the wine is her way of dealing. Looking at it now, I realize that drinking isn't any worse than Dad running away to hide at the hospital to escape the hell of watching his family come apart.

I stare at the ceiling, listening to her shallow breathing and my heartbeat in my ears. The winter sun pours in the window, and for once, I wish it was raining. Raining it more fitting for a day like this. Sunshine is too ironic, like nature's way of reminding me that none of us mean as much as we'd like to believe. When we're all gone, the sun will still shine, and the birds will still sing.

After a while, I feel Mom stir, and I turn my face to hers. She touches my cheek and pushes my hair back from my eyes. "I'm sorry I haven't been much of a mother lately."

I squeeze her other hand gently before letting it go. "It's no big deal. I don't think I've been a very good daughter," I say. "Or sister."

"You've done all you can, Cindy. We're all just tired. I'm tired. Tired and numb and hopeless." Mom turns her face to the ceiling and sighs. We're all going to end up like Audrey. Or Grandma."

"We don't know that Grandma—"

"We do. Let's not pretend."

Now the tears do come. I may have run out of tears for Audrey, but Mom saying this about Grandma makes it real. Of course, we all knew it was the most likely scenario when we could no longer get in touch with her. Her house was empty when Dad and I went over there to check on her. Untouched like she'd just stepped out to the supermarket or the post office.

Dad took what food was left there—he made me promise not to tell Mom. That day, I decided to believe she'd been taken to one of those FEMA camps and was safe and sound there.

"Your father is playing with fire," Mom goes on. "If he continues going to the hospital, it's only a matter of time until he becomes infected, as well.

"I never knew there could be anything worse than death."

I roll over and hug Mom. The smell of wine is a perpetual cloud around lately. "We have to be strong, Mom. And smart."

"Audrey was both of those things," she whispers as I pull away. "It's only a matter of time for the rest of us."

I go back to my room, unwilling to hear anymore, close the door behind me, and move to the window to look out. I would love to go outside and run, or feel the solid impact of a soccer ball against my laces. I would love to feel the sharp chill of the January air in my lungs and the too-bright sun on my face.

I would love to get out there and smell the cleanness of the ocean instead of the stink of death that hangs constantly in the air like a warning.

Everything out there looks ...off. The neighborhood is nearly empty—there are maybe a dozen families left in Sawgrass Flats. The lawns are brown and ignored. The silence is broken at irregular intervals by helicopters beating the air or gunshots.

My God, I've become so used to those noises that I barely notice them anymore.

CHAPTER 20

February 9
Nick

I'm trying to draw because the internet is down again, but my mind is blocked of everything but ugliness and dull, constant dread. Lines bleed from the end of my pen, creating chaotic scenes—a monster with a skull face and the figure of a hot girl. Behind her are swirls of smoke, but nothing definitive or familiar. I tear the page from my tablet, wad it up and toss it onto the floor, then collapse back onto my bed. I consider finishing the last of the weed I have hidden under the paints and brushes in my art bag but decide I'll save it for when I sneak over to Cindy's. She could use it, after everything she's been through. Besides, why waste it out of boredom? Who knows when I'll ever get any more?

Mom's been freaking out because Miles hasn't been home in three nights. She spoke to him on his cell the first night and he claimed he'd be back the next morning, but nothing. No more calls, or texts. I'm torn between thinking he's dead (or infected) or else, he's taken off for somewhere safer, leaving Mom and I to take care of his screaming brat, who must be napping because the house is eerily silent.

That silence is quickly broken by a crash. I jump, my heart pounding, and sit upright on my bed, looking around. Micah is shrieking at the top of his lungs now—Mom's break from his wailing is over.

But what the hell was that sound? I go to the window, but there's nothing to see out there but weeds taking over the back lawn, and our pool that's turned green with algae and ridden with dead leaves.

Mom's screaming now, as well, and my stomach tightens up. I sprint to the hall, but a harsh male voice spewing a stream of curses stops me in my tracks. It's not Miles, although it sounds like they share a similar vocabulary of four-letter words.

Another voice growls, "Check the rest of the fucking house. There's more than one kid here."

I can only assume they noticed a photograph downstairs. More sounds of footsteps on the hardwood, now; there must be three or people soldiers in our house.

"There's nobody else here," Mom's voice is shrill and frantic. "What do you want with us? We're not infected!"

"Maybe the other one's already dead."

"Probably, but check, anyway."

Micah's blubbering has reached a level even I've never heard.

"Shut that little fucker up, Jones."

"Don't touch him!" Mom yells, followed by a couple more loud thuds. I want to go to them, to stop whatever terrible thing is happening down there, but I can't make myself do it. I'm so scared and confused.

I dart back into my room, my heart thudding so hard and fast that I dry heave against the back of my fist. I grab my sketch tablet from the bed and smooth the covers to make it look as though nobody has been there, then slip into my closet.

Stupid. The closet is the first place anyone with half a brain will look. But there's nowhere else. I slide the double doors closed behind me and look around, my eyes straining against the darkness.

Up above my head, there's access to the attic that I'd nearly forgotten about. When I was about six, I went through an entire summer terrified of that hole. My cousin, who was an asshole, by the way, convinced me that a little troll lived in the attic and climbed through that access in the middle of the night to watch me sleep. Finally, Dad got enough of my sleeping at the foot of his and Mom's bed. He brought in a ladder and took me up to the attic through that access to show me that the scariest thing up there was the air handler and a few cobwebs.

I plant one foot on a low shelf and the other on the opposite wall and heave myself upward, careful not to make any more noise than I have to. I carefully lift the plywood access panel and push it aside, leaving just enough space for me to shimmy through. Then try to heave me up.

It's a struggle and I'm afraid I might not be able to do it. I've lost some of the strength I had when I was running and playing soccer. I haven't eaten since last night—I want to conserve what food we have left, just like I want to save my pot.

I hang there for a moment, my socked feet slipping against the wall without any traction. The footstep grow louder, echoing down the hallway outside my bedroom. I take a deep breath and tug myself upward, the muscles in my shoulders and arms screaming.

Then I'm up. I hear my bedroom door open just as I replace the access panel.

I squat there in the low side of the attic, afraid to move, sucking in cold, stale air. My thighs shake, and I want to change positions, but I don't dare move yet. Below, I can hear the soldier stalking around my bedroom, shuffling through my things.

The closet door opens, and hangers slide across the bars, scraping, metal on metal. My breath catches in my throat, and I wait for that panel to be thrown back, exposing my cowardly, trembling ass.

I feel something crawl across the back of my hand, and I cringe, but leave it. I hate spiders, but I'm not risking any movement.

Then heavy footsteps again, but now the sound is moving away from me.

"Anything?"

"Nothing. Nobody else here."

I remain inside the attic, shivering, for a while after the house becomes silent again. Then slowly, I open the access panel and ease myself back down into my closet. Cautiously, I step out into my bedroom, and then to the hallway.

I go into Mom and Miles's bedroom across the hall. Crouching, I move to the window that overlooks the front lawn and the street below. The house opposite ours belongs to the Smiths, a middle-aged couple who seem much younger than their ages. Evelyn Smith is a sharp-tongued artist who is (or was) constantly jogging along the streets in our neighborhood. She even challenged me to a race last summer. She kept up pretty well, but I ended up outrunning her. Had to—pride wouldn't let me lose to a sixty-year-old woman, no matter what kind of shape she was in.

Steve Smith is muscular and blond. He's a pediatrician who spends more time at the golf course than examining little kids. They have money and don't mind showing it off.

But it doesn't look like money matters anymore.

A soldier dressed in black riot gear kicks in the Smith's front door and four more follow him inside, rifles raised and ready.

In a moment, Steve and Evelyn are forced out onto their brown, overgrown lawn, guns shoved in their faces. Both are dressed as though they are heading to the country club, Steve's hair perfect, Evelyn's makeup perfect. Her diamond earrings glint in the sunlight.

Evelyn is shouting something, but I can't make it out. One of the soldiers slams the butt of his rifle against the side of Steve's head, sending him to his knees.

There's more shouting, but I still can't understand what's happening. One thing is obvious—one soldier is getting extremely agitated. He thrusts his rifle in Evelyn's face. Steve must say something else and another soldier kicks him in the ribs.

What the hell's happening? All those stories about martial law and government-sanctioned murders are true. The Shamblers are the least of our worries.

A soldier grabs a fistful of Evelyn's hair and forces her to her knees next to her husband. Both of them place their hands behind their heads. Something in my heart or in my brain knows what's about to happen. I need to look away but can't.

The shots are dull and decisive as Steve Smith's brains are blown all over Bending Reed Avenue.

The world gets black and splotchy in front of my eyes and I slide down the wall, on the verge of passing out. I bite the inside of my lip, hoping the pain might jar me back into awareness. I take several deep breaths and then move back to the window in time to see the Smith's limp bodies being loaded into the back of some sort of military transporter.

I run back to my room and pack some jeans, underwear, warm shirts, and socks into a backpack. I throw my sketch tablet and pencils in on top of that, followed by the scant remains of my pot. I then take my iPad and finally the small stack of photos I have of Dad, Mom, and me before Dad died and Miles moved in. Today, that life seems like something I dreamed.

I pull on my sneakers, grab my favorite black Patagonia jacket and my backpack, and head downstairs.

Since Micah came here, the only time I can remember the house being this quiet is when the kid's asleep at night. As I enter the kitchen, the heating unit kicks on and I nearly shit myself. Shaking my head at my stupidity, I take the few cans of food left in the cupboards and throw them into the backpack. There's also a box of angel hair and a jar of Newman's Own vodka sauce. In the fridge, I find a bottle of

Dasani and a half-block of cheddar cheese that's almost too dried out to eat.

I step into the foyer and what I see stops me dead in my tracks. There's fresh blood all over the floor and splattered on the wall just inside the front door. The dizziness hits me again, and I sink to my knees, fighting to stay conscious.

Is this Mom's blood? Is she dead like the Smiths?

Tears blur my vision as the reality dawns on me. I know I'll never see her again.

My stomach seizes up suddenly, and my body is wracked with dry heaves, unable to vomit anything up.

When that passes, I get back to my feet, my knees shaking, my nose and eyes running like crazy.

I open the front door and glance up and down the street. The military vehicle is down at the far end of the street. The soldiers have moved on to wreck what little remains of another family's lives. I step outside and look back at my house—the only place I've ever lived.

There's a red "X" sprayed painted and running on our front door, followed by the word "Cleared." Every other house on our street bears the small legend.

I sprint away, staying against the sides of the houses, near wildly growing plant beds, and behind the thick bases of live oaks until I'm out of the neighborhood. Once out, I keep to the woods along the sides of the nearly deserted roads. I'm still crying softly, my tears growing cold on my cheeks and the sides of my neck in the winter air.

I've lost everyone now. Dad, Mom, Grandma. Even idiot Miles, and Micah, who was only five, for Christ's sake. All that's left is Cindy. I have to get to her before these crazy fucking soldiers.

CHAPTER 21

♦

Cindy
February 15

So, Nick's mother is gone. My sister is gone. We've lost grandparents and stepparents and friends. Teachers we've loved are missing. Our lives have gone from planning our goals and dreaming about our futures to just trying to make it through the next day.

Maybe I should consider myself lucky—my parents are still here with me. Every morning I wake, stare up at the ceiling over my bed, and say a stupid little thanks to whoever or whatever is in control of things. Things have been strange since Audrey left us. Even worse once Nick arrived. We avoid her room. Dad cleaned it well enough to remove most of the odor, then closed it up, locking it and then hiding the key from me and Mom (like we'd ever want to go in there now).

Nick spends most of his time sitting on the floor, his back against the end of my bed, sketching. He hasn't said very much about losing his mother, and I'm not ready to push it. Instead, we listen to whatever comes on shuffle on my iPod, and he shows me how to draw things—monsters, fairies, animals. I could draw for one hundred years and never get much better than I am right now, I'm afraid. Nick's patient with my lack of artistic talent, but he's also extremely distracted. Even when we start making out, he stops before we get very far. He's being careful, but there's a part of me that feels a little hurt. That's the silly teenage girl in me who refuses to mature. You'd think witnessing society crumble would make me grow up a little quicker.

The house stays dim, although the day is bright and crisp. We've boarded up all the windows since he fled his neighborhood and told us about the soldiers. Then, we spray-painted the "CLEARED" symbol on our front door to make them think our place has been searched and emptied of survivors.

Two nights ago, we also moved in the cover of shadow and painted that same symbol on the rest of the front doors along our street—both those belonging to abandoned homes as well as those that are still inhabited. Maybe the soldiers will bypass our neighborhood, at least for a while.

Mom is like a ghost, passing from room to room. She appears for our scraped-together meals, and rations her remaining booze. She says little, and her eyes wear the permanent brownish bruises of a woman who will never recover from what she's lost. I feel as though she's already gone, just like Audrey was during her final days in the house. Dad is holding together as best as he can. He's given me a gun to keep near me at all times—his paranoia over the government has become as bad as his fear of the infected.

And much to my mortification, he's also presented Nick and me with condoms.

"I remember what it was like to be young," he says, shoving the box at Nick, whose face turns as red as a stop sign. "Don't be embarrassed. Be careful. But don't take this as a blessing to start screwing every chance you have."

"You sound like a PSA, Dad," I mutter, hoping to alleviate the shame. It doesn't.

February 18
Nick

I never dream about Mom, Miles, or Micah. When I dream, it's about Dad, and he's here now, and he knows what to do about surviving this epidemic. He's there like he's never left, level-headed, unafraid.

"I've seen the worst there is, Nicky. I've seen death. It's not as bad as people claim. You get through it," he says, his dream voice lilting and worry-free. "Some things are worse than death."

When I wake, I'm alone, unsure of where I am, darkness as thick as a blanket. I sit up and remember where I am—the sofa in the home of my former girlfriend/current Shambler and current girlfriend/possibly last girl on Earth.

I want to go upstairs and crawl into the bed with Cindy, but don't get any ideas. I just need to be near someone. When I'm down here, and everyone else is upstairs asleep, I feel I'm the only one left. Deep in the middle of the night, I believe I hear the moaning and screaming of the Shamblers. I hope I'm just imagining things, otherwise, they're coming up to the house at night. Like they smell the living inside.

February 22
Cindy

"So, do you think anyone will actually eat this?" I say, holding up a tiny can of potted meat. We're inside Mr. Howard and Mr. David's kitchen. Amazingly, most of the abandoned houses in Sawgrass Flats haven't yet been looted. Maybe there's a sense of community left inside the few of those who remain. But you've got to be realistic. I hate doing this, but these people are gone—they've fled or become infected. Either way, they've left behind the things they don't want or need.

Nick peeks around an open cabinet door. "I think it'll taste like caviar if we get hungry enough."

"I hate caviar." I wrinkle my nose and toss it into my backpack. Nick turns and kisses me.

"You've never had caviar," he says, smoothing my hair back from my face.

"Still. Fish eggs? Come on."

Mr. Howard and Mr. David's place is immaculate and the scent of the expensive aftershave Mr. Howard always wore still lingers. Daylight pours through the sheer drapes, making the home warm and inviting. On the refrigerator, there are photos of them at Niagara Falls, and on a cruise ship somewhere in the Caribbean. There's also a note, a reminder of a doctor's appointment, and a big, flowery greeting card that says, "To my best friend and lover. Together always." They were happy, and now they're both gone.

Most of us are doomed to the same fate. Life is so quickly summed up with a few photos, notes, and keepsakes. I'm staring too long at those things, and Nick snaps his fingers in front of my face.

"Don't do that, Cindy," he says, reading my mind. He opens the fridge, and the stink wafts out. The electricity has been shut off in this house for weeks.

"Shit! Close it," I shout.

"Wait," Nick says. "Check this out." He holds out a can of Coke. "There's a six-pack in here." I hold open my backpack, and he places five inside. The other one, he opens and takes a long, greedy drink.

"Here." He holds out the rather warm red can. I take a long gulp, savoring the sweetness. It feels like it's been a year since I had anything so sugary and wonderful.

"There are some things, too." I lean in next to him to take a look, shining my light in for a better look. On the little shelves on the inside of the door are Hershey Bars—six of them, three with almonds and three without. There are also pudding snacks in vanilla and butterscotch flavors.

"No wonder Mr. David was so chunky," I say.

"I guess," Nick agrees. Then he pulls out a large can of Redi Whip. "I wonder what they did with this?" He raises his eyebrows and leers at me, but even when he leers, he looks kinda hot.

"Let's not think about it." I push the fridge door closed.

We search through the rest of the kitchen, and then move from room to room, looking for anything we might be able to use in some way. We take batteries from remotes, just in case they might have a little juice left and candles—these guys must've loved scented candles.

But when Nick gets to the master bedroom, I stop him. "Let's just leave that room, okay?"

"How come?"

"Just a little act of respect, I suppose. It's none of our business."

Nick shrugs and moves away. "Okay."

We hit three more houses on the street before dark started to fall. Of course, daylight or darkness makes no difference to Shamblers—they're not vampires. But darkness makes it tougher on the living. Get a Shambler on your trail, fall over a lawn chair or sprinkler head, and that's that. They'll have their rotting teeth into your throat before you can say, "Oh, shit." Worse, using a flashlight is a dead giveaway to the living.

The take from the other homes is scant. More candles, a can of tuna in oil (yuck!), two packs of ramen noodles, a box of microwave popcorn (only good when there's electricity), a couple of envelopes of Kool-Aid—cherry and grape. Cheese with a skin of mold that can be cut away, and saltines that are only a little stale. And the best find of all—a big bottle of Jaegermeister, still three-quarters full.

"I think we should keep that one to ourselves," Nick suggests.

I agree. If Mom gets a hold of it, it'll be gone in a night.

February 25
Cindy

After a funky dinner of Ramen noodles and canned tuna, and canned pineapple for dessert, Dad calls us into the den. Mom's moping around because her wine supply is getting low, and maybe I should offer her the Jaeger, but decide against it. Not so much out of selfishness, but out of concern. She's drunk round the clock, lately. Running out of booze might do her some good.

After weeks of not noticing him, I realize Dad's looking so weary that my heart breaks. The circles under his eyes are deep and he's lost a lot of weight. He stands in front of a dark television, and the room is lit with the candles we scrounged from the other houses on the street.

So, it's the dreaded family meeting. I imagine Audrey there, smelling of pot and Blue Light perfume—too heavy— Mom and Dad pretending not to notice, hair a mess, me hating her because she got out for a few hours and lived without being someone's daughter and someone's sister. I've never had that, and I guess when I do, it's not going to be so pretty.

Dad takes a drink of one of the last Coors Lights he has in a cooler of melted ice. He makes a face, and I can't say that I blame him. I've tasted Coors Light and Bud Light and a few others, and it's all shit. But sometimes even shit makes you feel comforted, I guess.

"Okay. It looks like we're going to make other provisions in the coming weeks," he says. It sounds too formal. I want to tell him he's not talking to an audience, just me and Mom and Nick. There's no selling us.

Mom sips what she has left and looks so unhappy that I want to get away from her.

"Is leaving our home the answer, Ben?"

"If what Nick says is true, then the only option. I've been reading on the internet about what's happening in our neighborhoods. The military isn't being discriminatory. I don't know why, but I can't afford to take the chance."

"So we run away, then? Leave our home like a bunch of cowards?" Mom slurs.

"You have a better idea, Meg?"

I want to take Nick's hand, go upstairs, and hide until all of this is over and things are normal again. School's open. Soccer's stressful. Audrey's a bitch. If I've learned anything it's never complain over the little nuisances. There's always something worse out there, whether you believe it or not.

Mom scowls and doesn't reply. Finally, I break the awkward silence and ask, " So, what do we do?"

"I've been looking at heading to the mountains. Mike had a cabin in the Blue Ridge Mountains. They never used it because his kids didn't like it up there. They went a few times, but there was no internet connection and the cell service was spotty, at best. Those things don't matter now. What does matter is that it's way off the beaten path. With food, wood for heat, and the necessities, we could make it up there without worrying about the government coming in and taking us out. And the population is so low that the infected shouldn't be an issue."

Mike was Dr. Jacobs, his kind face a million years in the past.

Nick squeezes my fingers and sighs. "So, how do we get there?"

"We pack all we can and travel at night," Dad says. "We get out of town and then we stick to the back roads."

"But how do you know where Dr. Jacobs' place is? We've never been up there," I ask.

"No. But he gave me a few things before he turned." Dad moves to his battered briefcase. He flicks open the latch and then removes a crumpled map that looks to have been printed from a computer and a key on a corkscrew keychain.

...just before he turned...

Is he wandering around, a drooling monster in the Pastures now?

"We can get there. If we're careful and smart, we can get there," Dad says. He unfolds the map and traces a crooked line from the coast of South Carolina to the mountains of western North Carolina. "It's an easy drive. We'll travel to Greenville to refuel and gather more supplies if we can. We're looking at least six hours on the road, if we're lucky. Maybe more. We'll travel at night."

I cut my eyes at Nick. "We've been careful and smart so far," I say, immediately regretting it. Not all of us have been so lucky.

"It's a bad idea, Ben," Mom says, her words no more than a sigh. She runs her fingers through her matted hair, and I know at that moment that she's lost all hope.

"We must do this. There's no other option," Dad says, folding the crumpled map and placing it back into the briefcase.

"Nick and I will start getting things packed into the X5," I say. "We can do this, Mom."

Mom doesn't say anything. I wonder if she hears me at all.

CHAPTER 22

March 1
Cindy

Mom pretends Audrey's out with friends. I'm not sure if she believes it or if it's just her way of coping. Either way, it scares the hell out of me. I believe she's having some sort of breakdown.

Nick and I managed to find two unopened bottles of red and a half-finished bottle of white for her when we went to gather supplies this morning, but her mood remains insufferable.

"It's stupid to leave here," she bitches. "Audrey will be home and we'll be gone. I'm not going. Absolutely. Not. Going." She takes a long drink of the red. "Not until Audrey gets home."

I mention it to Dad, and he assures me she'll be fine. It's a reaction to the stress she's encountered with Audrey's transformation.

I want to argue with him that we haven't gone insane yet, so why is she so weak? But he looks so weary that I just nod and let him rest.

Several nights ago, I managed to pry from Dad the reason why he stays at the hospital so long. I'd assumed he was hiding from what our home and our lives had become. Mom's a drunk. Audrey's a zombie.

I'm not sure what I am anymore.

But Dad's told me he has two patients remaining in the hospital. Both are in their final days, but he's not the kind of man who leaves those who depend on him. He isn't an oncologist, but all the cancer docs in town are either deceased, changed, or just gone.

Dad and I are close, and some things don't have to be spoken aloud. He won't leave these patients behind, but he may end up "helping" them out.

It's pretty shitty having survived a worldwide epidemic just to be dying of cancer, but things are pretty shitty all the way around these days.

The helicopters are flying over at less frequent intervals now—maybe the "authorities" have become convinced that Sawgrass Flats is a ghost town now. For the most part, it's true. Nick and I have managed to get enough canned and instant foods, batteries, medicines, and other first-aid supplies that will hold us for at least six months. Mom's X5 has been pulled into the garage, so bandits or soldiers can't see how it's packed to the hilt with valuables.

It's funny. I never imagined people might get to the point where they'd kill for a package of twenty-five-cent Ramen noodles.

Once the BMW is packed, Nick and I return to my bedroom. Mom's passed out on the sofa where Nick normally sleeps, so we leave her. And frankly, I have no interest in seeing her, anyway. Dad's sprawled on the bed on top of the covers, still in his lab coat, snoring lightly.

"Shhh," I whisper, taking Nick's hand, leading him to my bedroom. Nick closes the door behind us, and I flip on the lamp next to my bed.

"So?" he says a little sheepishly, the lamplight making his pale skin appear warm. He needs a haircut—his hair is nearly to his shoulders, but still thick and silky. I love touching it, and when he climbs onto the bed next to me, I plunge my fingers into it and pull him to me.

He returns my kisses eagerly, his work-roughened fingertips caressing and scratching my cheek.

I've been wanting him for days. And whether he likes it or not, Dad has all but given us permission to have sex, providing us with a jumbo box of condoms (ribbed for her pleasure, by the way, whatever that means).

"You have that bottle of Jaeger up here?" he asks, after a moment.

"It's in the bottom drawer of my dresser."

Nick crawls for the end of the bed like a silly kid, and bounds over to the dresser. He opens the middle drawer instead and begins sorting through my underwear.

"Not that drawer, jackass!" I protest, but not before he's taken out an especially lacy and feminine pair of pink bikinis.

"Wow! Why don't you wear these sometime?"

I snatch them from him, my face burning. "Because, they feel terrible."

I'm a cotton boy-shorts kind of girl. It's all about comfort for me. Besides, style is low on the list lately. I don't want to have to stop and dig my panties out of my ass while fleeing Shamblers.

"They're hot," he argues. "Hell, they're turning me on and you're not even wearing them...yet."

"Please!" I shove the panties back into the drawer, then bend down and find the bottle of Jaeger both excited and a little frightened to drink anything that strong.

I unscrew the top and take a long gulp, trying too hard to be bold. The taste is like licorice and Robitussin cough syrup and would've been better had it been chilled. Either way, I swallow it without gagging and pass the bottle to Nick. He downs a long drink like a pro. A nice play-off, I determine—he's no more a pro than I am.

"It's bad," I say, looking up into his eyes.

"An acquired taste," he whispers. Then he leans forward and kisses me, soft and tentative at first, just like the first time we kissed. The sugary drink glues our lips together. I taste his mouth, his tongue, warm and silky sweet, my hands coming up, caressing his chest through his t-shirt. His heart beats so fast that it frightens me at first until I realize my own heart is beating even faster.

Then he breaks the kiss and takes another drink of the liquor. I do the same, and the flavor isn't as bad the second time around. I place the bottle on the dresser behind us. My head is spinning already, and my stomach doesn't feel quite right. Nick kisses me again, his hard body pressing against me. I'm so aware of how he feels...lower. The hard knot there, pushing against my thigh, my crotch. Part of me wants to pull away, afraid.

But part of me wants to feel more of him. I want to know what a boy is really like. I push myself against him, sighing into his hot mouth.

Nick pushes me back toward my bed and I just go, like some silly, mindless robot. I lie back and he is on top of me, his mouth on my mouth, on my throat. The knot in his jeans is larger, burning, and desperate. The place between my legs is the same. We thrust against each other, aching more and more. We're eager, yet frustrated by the confines of our clothes. Nick's hands explore my stomach under my shirt and bra. I smell his hair as it falls on my face, a mixture of sweat and some kind of men's shampoo. My fingers move to the waist of his jeans, daring to slip lower, brushing the brittle hairs there.

"Should I get that...box?" I don't want to say what the box is, for some reason.

Nick pulls back, resting on his hands above me. His face is beautiful at that moment, the light soft and warm orange, his hair too long and falling on his forehead and his cheeks. He considers things for a moment, then bends low and kisses me again.

"Don't."

"What?" Why am I so bummed? "Don't you want to do this?"

I want to do it, to get past it. I want to be beyond the fear and wonder of what the first time holds. I've heard so many things—pain, disappointment, sadness. Distance. I want it over with because if it's not now, one of us might not be here tomorrow.

Time's limited.

"I'm sorry, Cindy, but not now. Not like this."

"Like what?" I ask, trying to hide my annoyance.

"Drinking. I don't want to do this while we're drinking."

I'm getting it. Yeah, turns out I'm not superhuman. I get slow when I drink.

"All right," I whisper.

Nick rolls off of me and we stare up at the ceiling.

"You're not mad, are you?"

"No." I lie.

His hand finds mine, and he weaves his fingers between mine.

"I want to do this right. Do you understand what I mean?" he says, turning his face to mine.

"Not really, but it's okay," I tell him.

"There's only this one time. I want to do this the right way because it matters."

It matters. I don't know how to respond. So, I just squeeze his fingers between mine and try not to cry. I wasn't sure anything mattered in the world we now live in except just surviving.

After a while, we fall asleep on my bed, fingers still entwined. Outside, a shambled screams out, and dream it's Audrey, still screaming through the walls of her bedroom.

CHAPTER 22

March 7
Cindy

Mom is gone.

I don't know what else to say about it. She was gone when I woke. Dad had already left by the time I noticed, hiding behind helping the handful of people who are clinging to something that's not quite life, but not death, either.

The gun from Dad's desk drawer is gone also.

I can't say I'm surprised by this. The fact is, I really don't know how I feel about it. I don't know if I feel anything at all.

I don't mean to come across as cold, but it's like I'm just numb. Numb, blind, and stumbling around inside some terrible dream from which I cannot wake.

Nick and I search the neighborhood, but there's no sign of Mom. She left us on foot, with only the clothes she had on. She didn't take her heavy coat, although the temperature was not climbing above fifty most days. The weather in March has always sucked—a tease of spring one day, sleet the next. The nights are frigid and miserable and Mom's cold-natured like me.

Dad doesn't know. The cell connection is shaky, but it doesn't matter. I haven't tried to call him. Not yet.

Nick and I walk the empty streets of Sawgrass Flats, no longer very concerned over the military flyovers. Ground patrols are infrequent, at least around here. Maybe Nick's idea of marking the houses as "cleared" worked to keep the soldiers out.

The sun beats down, a kiss of warmth on the tops of our heads, balancing the chilly breath of late winter that numbs our cheeks, noses, and chins.

The stink of rot and death has either diminished, or else I've become so used to it that I no longer notice.

Nick carries a baseball bat, and I'm just looking around at the dead houses, the dead lawns. A little dog barks. It sounds close, but the animal has become too shy to come out and be seen.

"Do you think she went out for supplies?" Nick asks. He knows better than that, but he's trying to shield me from more pain. I appreciate it, but it's not realistic or helpful. It's just pretending.

I shrug. "She's never lifted a finger to help. Not since Audrey got sick." I sound angrier than I intend, but I am angry. Nothing's mattered to Mom since Audrey was bitten. Dad and I always played second fiddle to Audrey.

Sure, it's the same way with Dad and me, but he didn't show it. He didn't rub it in their faces and make them feel excluded from some sort of fabulous, secret club like Mom and Audrey did.

I'm a bitter bitch, okay?

I want to believe Mom selected one of these empty houses. She went inside and just finished things off.

I could see that being her way. She'd know that we wouldn't search every house, every closet, or attic. She'd make the choice of going where we wouldn't find her. What she went to do was a private thing. Secret, and she would find a secret place to do it. Plus, she's too goddamned vain to leave herself where we might find her—looking less than perfect.

Frankly, it sucks that she's taken our gun to use it for her own selfish purposes.

Nick takes my hand, and I let him although I don't really feel like holding his hand or talking. I want to blow up and be pissed off at the world for being so shitty. I want to be pissed off at Mom for leaving, and at Dad for not being able to save us like I always imagined he could. I'm pissed at Audrey for first being a bitch and then a Shambler.

I'm pissed at myself for being pissed.

Worse than anything else, I'm pissed at myself for crying, which is what I'm suddenly doing. It breaks like a stupid floodgate and I just sink to the pavement, nearly pulling Nick down with me.

"Cindy!" Nick cries, dropping to his knees next to me. "Are you okay?"

He means physically, I know that, but I can't help but snap at him.

"No, I'm not fucking okay! My Mom's gone! My sister's a zombie and my Dad's losing it, I'm pretty sure."

Nick take my face in his hands, the palms of his fingerless gloves warm and soft, the pads of his fingers brushing my cheeks, rough as sandpaper. He makes me look at him although I don't want to. I don't want him to see me blubbering like one of those girls at school who always cried at the drop of a hat.

"Don't look at me," I whisper, my lips and eyes feeling too hot and swollen.

"Don't hide your tears from me," Nick says. He smudges them away with his thumb, smiling, his own eyes shining with tears.

"Please. It's stupid."

"It's not stupid. It's not! Do you think I don't cry? Shit, I cry over nearly every night, Cindy. On the sofa of your living room, lying in the dark. Sometimes, I scream into the sofa cushions. I get it out. It's the only way I get through the days sometimes."

"You do?" I'm not sure I believe him. He's never shown any signs of being anything less than perfect. Strong, level-headed. Awesome.

He smiles. "Of course. What? Do you think I'm some kind of tough-ass?"

"Sort of," I whisper, blushing.

"Well, I'm not. And neither are you. Face it." It stands and pulls me to my feet. "Come on."

Slowly, we begin moving down the street again. I lean into his side, loving his warmth. But I still feel helpless.

"We're not going to find her, you know. At least, not alive."

"I know. But it's only right to pretend we might, isn't it?"

"I guess so," I agree. Maybe it is right to pretend. It's the only way we can retain some facade of humanity when so much of it is already gone.

I find the note before Dad gets home. Mom left it on the fridge, stuck there on the door between photos of me and Audrey—some recent, and others when we were quite small. It's secured by a little magnetic heart that bears the legend, "World's Best Mom."

I don't like what it says and decide quickly that Dad doesn't need to know what Mom thinks of him. It's best to let her go. It helps him let her go.

I'm afraid of how he's going to take it. At what point will he finally break? Or is he already broken and just going through the motions of surviving, like most of the ones who remain?

March 10
Cindy

I wonder how many things Dad can hold inside before he bursts. Just like his reaction when Nick and I tell him about Mom.

"Are you sure?"

"Yes," is all I answer. I don't mention the note. I just can't. Maybe Mom wasn't deliberately being hurtful, but still, it is. Even if much of what she wrote is true.

"Did you look for her?" Dad asks.

"We looked," Nick tells him. "Every house on the street, Mr. Scott."

"We couldn't decide how long she'd been gone," I say.

Dad nods. He sinks onto the kitchen stool, slumps over the counter, and buries his face into his shaking hands.

He sobs, a loud, harsh noise.

It takes me a moment before I realize he's actually crying. My dad. Crying. I'm so shocked, I don't know how to react. I touch his shoulder, timid, as if he's suddenly so fragile that a simple caress might break him.

"I'm sorry, Dad. I'm sorry I didn't notice she was gone!"

Now, I'm crying, too. Again.

He gropes blindly at me and roughly snatches me into his arms. I bury my face against his stubbly jaw, smelling the faint scent of his aftershave or soap—the same comforting scent I remember from days when I had scraped knees and bumps on my noggin. It has always been Dad for those things, never Mom. Mom was for buying the right shoes for the Sadie Hawkins dance and teaching me which fork to use (even when we're having pizza).

"It's okay," he whispers against my hair. "It's going to be all right."

"It's not!" I cry. "Things are going to shit and we can't stop it." My eyes find Nick standing awkwardly across the kitchen, chewing his bottom lip.

The panic I felt when I collapsed on the road earlier returns, threefold. Things were never supposed to be like this. When the news reports first started, I never thought our little family would be touched by this thing. Things like this happened to other families, in other cities. Big cities. Not silly little communities of only a few thousand people.

Once upon a time, I believed we were immune to tragedy.

CHAPTER 23

March 13
Cindy

The focus has become getting away from Palmdale. Dad grieves over Mom just like he grieves over Audrey. Silently. Shielded himself from Nick and me. I've gotten very good at things I never thought I'd be good at. Breaking into locked houses. Siphoning gasoline from the abandoned cars left in the driveways and garages all along the avenue.

We'll need at least five good canisters of gasoline, Dad says, for travel, and then for the generator once we get into the mountains. We have eight. And food and water? We have dried pasta, bouillon, canned tuna, and powdered milk. You name it. We're not exactly eating like royalty, but we're not starving. Plus, Dad says we'll be able to hunt once we get to Dr. Jacob's cabin.

Dad looks for Mom every morning and every evening. He says he taking a walk, but I know he's searching for her body. More for closure than anything else.

We all could use some sense of closure. Nick feels his own mother is dead, too. I'm not sure what's worse—knowing your parent took her own life out of weakness, or knowing some slime ball posing as a savior decided your parent was just another causality of war.

Dad printed out a calendar and taped it to the microwave door. We're out of here in a week. On it he's created a sort of "to-do" list—the important things we need to be sure to tackle in the remaining seven days here in Palmdale.

I feel a little sad to leave, but there's too much hurt around here. It awaits me in every corner and at every turn. It sucks because so many wonderful things happened on the same floors where my feet are now planted, but those things are shut off from me now.

It's like watching a movie that you never want to end.

March 14
Cindy

Dad makes his famous (or is it infamous, by now) tuna casserole for dinner. With it, he opens the last bottle of Mom's burgundy.

"Red doesn't go well with fish," he says, swirling the dark liquid around in our best crystal, raising his eyebrows in a faux-snooty manner that's not like him at all. "But what the hell?"

He then pours up two more glasses for me and Nick. "We're not driving tonight, are we?"

"No, sir. Not tonight," Nick says, taking his glass from the counter. Candles flicker around the room. The electricity is faulty this evening—something that's happening more and more frequently. It'll be on for an hour and off for three. Of course, we have the generator, but the weather's not especially cold tonight, so the gasoline will be saved for later. Besides, it's already packed into the back of the SUV, along with the fuel canisters, boxes of food and blankets, and other necessities. That's day four on Dad's list, by the way, but it's done. Everything is done.

Almost.

Dad's iPod is docked in a cheap-assed "boombox," as he calls it. It looks like something straight out of the 1980s, with a handle and big, thumping speakers. I don't ask where he found this monstrosity, but it works well enough—despite Dad's taste in music.

He's on a Fleetwood Mac kick tonight. My only knowledge of Fleetwood Mac is Stevie Nicks' White Witch on a couple of episodes of *American Horror Story*.

But Nick digs it big time. "My dad loved this," he says, his face brightening in the dim light. He takes my hand and spins me around the kitchen, oddly jubilant to the haunted strains of "Rhiannon."

"You don't have to try so hard to get on his good side," I tease, cutting my eyes to Dad. "You're already in."

Nick laughs. "I'm not trying to get on anyone's good side."

"Seriously."

"Seriously," he says, spinning me once again.

I stumble against a kitchen stool, and Dad grabs my shoulder to steady me. "Careful."

We sit down to dinner at the counter. It seems too strange to use the table now that there are two empty spaces there.

"This isn't going to be as good as usual. The chips were stale so I substituted saltines," Dad says, helping a big serving onto a plate. He passes it to me.

My appetite has been nonexistent lately but roars back once the smell of the casserole hits me. My stomach rumbles and I take a greedy bite without waiting on Nick or Dad. Frankly, tonight, Emily Post can kiss my ass.

Once we're all served, Dad then refills our wine glasses. I'm still surprised by this, but just enjoy it and say nothing. I love the way it makes me feel—so unlike the Jaeger and the rum, which went straight to my head too quickly. The wine is a slow and easy warmth that spreads through my chest and then my brain. It's rather lovely, I decide and wish we had another bottle to share.

"I don't think we'll have a lot of trouble getting out of town," Dad comments between bites.

"I haven't heard the choppers in a few days," Nick says. "Maybe they've written Palmdale off."

"Either that or nearly everyone is dead," I suggest.

"Maybe," Dad says. "I'm not sure which is more troubling."

"To hell with the military," Nick snarls. "I hope they're all dead."

Dad pushes his noodles back and forth across his plate, thoughtful.

"Well, considering how things were going, it wouldn't be an altogether bad thing. I just never imagined it would be acceptable to murder Americans," I say.

"It's not acceptable," Dad says quietly. "But the nation we knew is gone. For all we know, there's no longer a government. There's just some scared, crazy people out there fighting to survive."

"We're fighting to survive, Dad. But we haven't killed anyone to do it," I say.

"But it doesn't mean we won't have to," Nick whispers. He takes a long sip of his wine, his eyes meeting Dad's over the edge of his glass.

"You're exactly right, Nick. It's scary, but it's something we must be prepared to do."

My head's swirling gently, and I'm enjoying the growing buzz I'm getting, so I really wish we'd move on to a more positive subject. "Well, that's the reason for getting out of town, isn't it? To be away from the dangers of not only the Shamblers, but also the dangers of the living."

"Exactly," Dad agrees. "So after I make one more visit to the hospital in the morning, we'll go. You two make sure you take everything you want to take with you. And don't forget to gather your textbooks. We're not going on vacation."

"Do you really have to go back to the hospital?" I ask.

"Cindy. We've talked about this."

"But what are you going to do? With the ones who are left, I mean?" I ask, hating the whining tone my voice is now taking.

"I'm going to allow them to make their own choices. Plus, Jolee and Sylvia are staying. Along with Dr. Marcus and Dr. Edwards."

"Why would they choose to do that?" I ask. The interest I once had in sticking my neck out to help others is long gone. Now, all I'm concerned with is making the three of us stay alive.

"None of them have family. It's their choice to remain there."

My stomach does a strange, slow roll. Jolee had a young daughter, I remember. A little doll-faced redhead. A mini version of her mom. "Oh," is all I say.

We finish our meal without any more discussion, Stevie Nicks' sweet, raspy voice filling our lifeless, shadowy kitchen.

When we move to the living room, Nick stokes the fire to get it going again, and the room quickly becomes toasty. The wine has won out over my wakefulness, and I'm extremely drowsy and goofy-headed.

The three of us sleep in there together for warmth, Dad on the sofa, Nick and I nestled into sleeping bags on the floor on either side of the room. Dad's pretty liberal-minded but there's an old-fashioned streak in him that's a mile wide, and Nick doesn't dare place his bag near mind. After a quick peck on the lips, we bed down.

Groggy, I stare up at the ceiling, the dancing flames from the fireplace painting the world a soft, warm orange, and fight back another bout of tears. This the only home I've ever known, but tomorrow, once we pile into the SUV and pull away, I know I'll never see it again.

CHAPTER 24

March 15
Cindy

Beware the Ides of March.

I think this when I notice the date, but cannot remember where I first heard it. Then it dawns on me. Julius Caesar in sophomore English. It seems like a thousand years since I stepped foot in school.

Nick and I were still sleeping when Dad left for the hospital for the final time. When we finally woke, we moved around the house, frightened, anxious, and also giddy with excitement over the new possibilities and new challenges that await the three of us.

Now, Nick lies back on my bed, attempting to log on to the internet with his iPad, as I go through my drawers and shelves one more time. I don't want to find out later that I've left something important behind.

We've packed the X5 to the gills. The only things I've chosen not to take are senseless clothing—uncomfortable shoes, and dresses. Fancy-assed blouses. Pantyhose. I find a pair of nude-colored hose—the kind that comes in an egg-shaped box—in the bottom of my underwear drawer and toss them in the general direction of the wastebasket.

"I won't be sad if I never have to squeeze myself into another pair of hose," I tell him.

"So, you're seeing some upsides to this end-of-the-world thing, then," Nick answers.

I smile. "Maybe a little."

Outside, the day is bleak. Clouds moved in overnight, and it rained steadily most of the day. We haven't seen anyone in days. No Shamblers. No survivors. Just nothing.

I step inside my closet and begin going through what's left of my clothes again. Nearly everything I feel is worth taking is already packed into an overstuffed garbage bag. We've opted not to use the luggage—bags are easier to pack into the tight rear area of the BMW.

"I'm on," Nick calls, excited.

"Really?" It's been two days since we were last able to find a signal. I pop out of the closet and leap onto the bed next to him.

He signs onto Instagram. None of his contacts have been active in days. Then Vine. There aren't very many new videos there, either. The few that are shared are stupid clips of jerks teasing Shambles, enticing them into a chase. There's a clip of a kid who looks to be about ten years old. He's following an infected girl, about my age. Her top is off, and she's just lurching around, her small boobs beginning to show signs of rot. The kid pokes at her nipples with a long twig, once and then again. The end of the twig sinks into her softened, decayed flesh, right through the nipple.

The unseen camera operator howls with laughter and the little video star cackles and sprints, barely eluding the girl's claw-like grasp.

"Turn it off," I say, disgusted. I lie back on the bed and sigh. That girl could've been Audrey. Or me.

Nick places the iPad aside. "I'm sorry," he whispers.

"It's the world we live in, isn't it?"

"I'm afraid it is," he agrees. Then he places his fingers under my chin and tilts my face up. He kisses me slowly, his lips brushing mine, his mouth opening, his tongue dancing with my tongue.

I draw back and bite his bottom lip playfully. My fingers walk down his chest to his stomach. Lower, over the front of his jeans. His eyes widen and he laughs as he presses upward against my hand.

"Nick," I begin. My face grows furiously hot before I even get all the words out. "I don't want to die a virgin."

Nick's sweet smile dissolves. "What? That's not going to happen."

"How do you know that? There's something terrible waiting on us around every stinking corner."

"That's why we're getting out," he argues.

"Still. It may be too late." I lie back on the bed again and stare at the ceiling.

"Don't be like that, Cindy," he says, leaning over me. His soft hair tickles the side of my face. He really could use a haircut, but honestly, his long hair is incredibly hot. He looks like a guy straight out of Seventeen Magazine, and I wonder suddenly what chance I might've had with him had I not been practically the last girl on earth.

He bends and kisses me again, but this kiss is something more. It's urgent and forceful, yet tender. He moves onto me, and I love the warmth of him, the gentle weight of his body on mine. He presses himself against me, his fingers sliding under my shirt, then my bra, awakening my nipples until they harden into little stones.

I help him tug his shirt over his head. He's gorgeous, but he's lost weight—we all have. And his skin is paler than he's ever been. We're children of the sun, but can't chance to be out in the sun very often. Getting away from Palmdale will change that, hopefully.

I fumble with the button of his jeans and slip my hand inside, grasping, stroking, until he whispers for me to stop.

We undress quickly in the shadowy afternoon light.

I'm not going to die a virgin, after all. At least I'll have that going for me.

March 18
Nick

I jump awake, my mind racing, and grab for the iPad to check the time. It is nearly three p.m. We'd fallen asleep holding each other, tucked beneath the soft weight of Cindy's down comforter, naked and looking extremely guilty if Ben were to show back up. Thankfully, the door is closed and locked—another glaring sign of guilt. I get up and dress, careful not to wake Cindy. The daylight coming through the window is dimmer, now, the shadows in the room long and heavy.

Cindy hears me moving around and wakes. She smiles as she brushes her tangled hair from her face, so beautiful that it makes my heart ache. There's nothing in her that reminds me of Audrey, with her light hair and eyes, but I still feel a little strange, being with her. I might've loved her long before I realized Audrey wasn't anything but a pain in the ass, and circumstances just brought us together.

Deadly epidemics have a funny way of changing a person's plans for the future, you know.

She climbs from the bed, naked, but still oddly modest considering the fact we just made love. She dresses quickly, her back turned to me, but I'm not complaining. The view is almost as nice as it is from the front. She's athletic and small, but firm. She looks strong, which is a very good thing. Ben and I have complained about her running, but honestly, it's for her to keep fit—and not just for the nice view. She can outrun a Shambler with no problem.

Shit, cardio is *Zombieland* rule number one, you know.

"You think Dad's back?" she asks.

"I don't know." We head downstairs, groping in the darkness. I hate that we've had to board up the windows. Like Cindy, I need to see the sunshine and want to feel its warmth pouring through the windows. In the kitchen, Cindy lights the nub of a candle and calls for her father.

Nothing. And it's obvious he hasn't been back yet.

"I really thought he'd be back by now," Cindy says, her voice shaking with worry. Our plans are to get out and on the road to the cabin before sunset.

I step out into the garage where the X5 sits, packed and waiting, and the cold jars me into full wakefulness. I grab a bottle of water from the box next to the door and take a long drink. It's relatively cold since the garage is so chilly, but tastes metallic and funky. Bottled water is tough to find lately —the supermarkets are picked clean, as are the Walmarts and the gas stations—so we've taken to refilling bottles with tap water as often as possible. There's a chance I'll have an upset stomach later on, but right now, I'm good at taking my chances.

"Maybe he got tied up," I suggest, but I'm thinking something worse. Lately, you just want help but think of something worse. Our entire lives have become a game of Worst Case Scenario.

Cindy sighs and sits down at the kitchen table, the candle flickering in front of her. She bites her lip like she does when she's afraid and determined not to show it. "Stupid of him to keep going back there," she mutters.

I touch her shoulder and sit down next to her. "It's not stupid. You'd do the same thing," I tell her. "You're just like him. You both just want to do what's right. You want to help."

"Wanting to help people isn't stupid."

She raises her eyes to mine and smiles sadly. "We're just wonderful people," she says, sarcastically.

"Yeah. Pretty wonderful," I agree, offering her the bottle of water. She takes a drink, then wipes her mouth with the back of her hand.

"Yuck." She wrinkles her nose.

"Tell me about it," I say. Then I offer, "Look. Let's give him an hour. If he's not back, we'll go to the hospital and check on him. Okay?"

"Yeah. Okay." Cindy nods, clearly perked up. "I'm probably just overreacting, anyway."

March 20
Cindy

Getting to the hospital is easier than I thought it would be. Nick and I decided to take bicycles—easier to outrun Shamblers and to get off the streets and into hiding, if necessary—but with the desolation of what used to be my hometown, we could've taken the M5 undetected. With the hospital only a few minutes away, Dad is always taking his chances either on foot, by bike, or in his car, if the streets appeared quiet on that particular day. Today it appears he's taken his car. I don't really blame him. It's cold out.

The sun's getting low, but we still have a couple of hours until dusk. My nose runs as we bike along, and the chilly air makes my eyes water. The dead world lies ahead of me blurry and unfocused.

The stink of the dead and the odors of everyday human life is gone—exhaust from automobiles, perfume or B.O. from people passing by, the grease of food cooking in the restaurants, smoke from fireplaces—all gone now. I smell the briny ocean, although the Atlantic lies a mile to the east of where we are.

I haven't been on this street since my last trip to the hospital, the night Audrey was bitten. There's a supermarket with the entire glass front crushed in. Trash has blown out into the nearly-empty parking lot—soda cans, potato chip bags, candy wrappers. A couple of cars remain in the lot, covered in a heavy blanket of grime and dust.

The BBQ restaurant Dad loved is boarded up as if for a hurricane. The familiar "CLEARED" sign has been sprayed on the plywood that covers the front entrance.

Here and there, cars and trucks sit abandoned, covered with filth, forgotten. On the far side of the street, we spot a Shambler, a teenage boy. He's wearing a Palmdale High football jersey, jeans that are falling nearly to his knees, and one sneaker. He stumbles with every other step because of his pants.

"Nick. Stop," I say, pulling to a halt.

Nick coasts to a stop next to me and we watch the kid, who's lurching along directionless, mouth agape, whitish eyes dull. His thick hair is screwed up into filthy spikes, untouched for quite a long while.

"Is that Tommy?" I ask. I'm not sure why I'm whispering.

"Yeah," Nick answers. "It's Tommy. He's number twelve."

several emotions hit me all at once. There's sadness for yet another one of us gone. There's the fear that either Nick or myself will be the next one. And finally, there is this dark, wretched feeling that I'm witnessing a weird kind of justice.

Part of me always felt it was Tommy Barker's fault that Audrey was infected.

Karma's a bi-otch, they say. And so am I.

Tommy stumbles on, no puffs of breath floating upward from his lips in the cold air as it does for me and Nick. Noticing how a seemingly living human is not breathing is one of the most jarring aspects of the N-Virus victims. That in itself proves they are indeed the walking dead.

I watch Nick's face as he watches Tommy stagger away from us, but I can't read his expression. Finally, I just put it out there. "He deserves it."

Nick shrugs. "Maybe. But do any of us deserve that?"

I push off. "Some of us do. What about those soldiers who took your mom? Surely you must believe they deserve this kind of ending. After what they did to you?"

"I suppose so," Nick says, peddling along behind me. He doesn't sound convinced. Nick's a lot more forgiving than I am.

We travel in silence, the hospital looming ahead of us, shadowy, most of the windows black against a graying backdrop of a cloudy late afternoon sky.

A voice inside my brain screams something isn't right as we approach the hospital's front entrance. There are less than two dozen cars scattered around the parking lot, and aside from Dad's Lexus, most appear they haven't moved in months. Around the big sliding doors, the weeds have gone out of control. The once-immaculate landscaping has gone to hell. Sprigs of brownish grass shoot up between cracks in the walking path. Everything is so eerily silent that I can hear my heart thudding inside my chest and pulsing in my ears. My throat clicks when I swallow as if I've eaten a mouthful of dust.

Something is burning—the rubber and plastic stink hits rise as we move closer to the building.

"Something's wrong, isn't it?" I whisper, wanting Nick to tell me that I'm just paranoid. That I'm nuts. Anything but that I'm right.

After a moment, Nick answers, "Difficult to tell from here. It's probably because there's no light." He doesn't sound very positive.

We ditch the bikes twenty yards in front of the front doors. It's impossible to detect movement inside—this entrance is also an emergency entrance and is covered to shield people from bad weather at the drop-off. It's as black as a cave there, weak overhead lights flickering like broken butterfly wings, never long enough to break the darkness.

We walk the rest of the way, and I'm chewing my bottom lip and fighting the urge to break into a sprint toward the door. Nick senses my unease and takes my hand. "Slow. Okay?"

So, he thinks something is off, too.

The sun is low and hidden behind the building, making it even colder in the shade. I shiver, and Nick squeezes my fingers tighter, trying his best to comfort me. Under the arched awning leading to the front doors, the lights flicker again, accompanied by a dry, electric buzz.

"Stop!" Nick hisses, yanking me backward.

Then I see it.

Sprayed across the glass doors is one word. "CLEARED."

"No!" I pull toward the doors, but Nick holds me back, his grip on my hand becoming painful as my fingers crush together.

"Don't! They could still be in there." Nick pulls me away from the doors and behind the skeletal shrubs that line the base of the building, snagging our coats on the prickly branches. "Shhh."

We wait a moment, but there's nothing but stillness and silence. My eyes tear up, and I blink hard to clear away the blurriness. My stomach clenches, nausea hitting in waves. Even when I first saw Audrey and her stupid mangled leg,

I've never been so stricken with dread. I wish I could run away, back home, and just start things over, rewind back my life to nine months ago.

But we have to go and see. We have to see what we already know, just to confirm it.

"Come on," Nick says, and we move around to the rear of the hospital. My mind races—in a few moments, we'll go inside and there will be Dad, in his coat, looking tired and pissed that we've shown up because it's too dangerous to stray very far from our house. He'll be fine. He'll be alive, and there to keep me safe like he always has been.

The emergency ambulance entrance is partially blocked by a fire and rescue truck that has been vandalized and stripped. A front tire is missing, a hose hangs from the gas tank like a thin, limp tongue lolling out onto the ground. The rear doors hang ajar. Everything that can be taken has been taken from inside.

We creep around toward the back door, scanning for movement, people living or dead.

The automatic sliding doors are stuck, leaving an opening about a foot wide. Nick peeks inside, then forces the doors apart. We step inside a deserted, dim hallway. Overhead, the fluorescent lights hum and flicker, the threat of complete uninterrupted darkness very real.

My mind races. Why does Dad continue to come here?

We move down the hall, more afraid than cautious. The only sounds are our sneakers padding dully on the floor and our breaths coming too fast. I want to vomit, I'm so afraid of what we're going to find. I silently curse Mom for taking our gun, something I've done on a semi-daily basis since she vanished.

We make a right turn into the main hall E.R. waiting area —empty. The last day I volunteered, months ago, when the N-Virus was still something we all thought we'd beat, pops into my head. How crowded it was. The stink of the sick.

There's a different smell now. It's coppery, ripe, familiar, unpleasant.

We find the first of the murdered behind the nurses' station—pretty Jolee has been shot in the head. Her eyes are wide, staring upward toward the ceiling. Drying blood frames her head like a wretched halo. Her expression is somewhere between horror and relief.

"Damn," Nick mutters, pulling me away. "They've been here."

I want to press my face against his chest and cry for her. What a goodhearted, funny, hard-working woman she was. The unfairness of it all.

I want to believe that Dad got out. That he is hiding somewhere, but my heart is breaking. I know what's awaiting me.

The few people who are left—the uninfected—have been executed as if they were Shamblers. It's hateful and indiscriminate. There's nobody coming to save us. They're just there to end things. Maybe their gift to everyone is making sure death is quick and final instead of a kind of horrible limbo.

Unable to control myself, I scream for my father. "Dad, it's me. Please come out!"

"Don't, Cindy. We don't know for sure—"

"Dad," I call out again.

There's a male nurse lying in the middle of the hall. Drying gobs of brain and bone scatter the wall behind him. I never knew his name, as it seemed he was always leaving as I was coming in, but I remember his dreamboat smile.

I tear my hand free of Nick's and start running, calling Dad over and over. I throw open every door I come to.

"Cindy. Don't be crazy!" Nick calls, sprinting after me. "This is too dangerous."

I ignore him and crash through the door leading to the stairway. I race up, taking two steps at a time. I'm crying, my nose clogged with snot, and my eyes again becoming hot and swollen. I'm shaking all over.

On the second floor are patient rooms and the pediatric ward. Smiling giraffes, dancing elephants, and insanely happy lions decorate the walls, but the ward is empty. No kids. No staff.

My frantic running slows to a jog. I'm puffing through my mouth, crying uncontrollably. The nurses' desk on this floor is deserted. The supply closet next-door has been pillaged.

I throw myself against the first door I come to and find an empty bed. The same with the next. Nick trails me, the gun up and ready.

"Dad?" I call again, no longer really expecting a response, but hoping for some sort of miracle.

Most rooms appear untouched for quite a while. Some have been cleaned, others left with beds unmade, sheets and pillows stained with blood. I.V. bags hang half-empty, lines left dripping slowly.

In the next room, an extremely elderly woman lies, her head off her pillow, one side of her skull crushed in. Blood is like spilled paint around tufts of cottony white hair and running down the side of the mattress onto the floor.

I do not step all the way into the room. There's nothing inside that I want to see up close.

It's two doors down that I find the things that will always haunt my nightmares.

Dad. My poor, gentle, beautiful father. My hero. My protector.

He's slumped over a vague shape in the bed, a youngish man, emaciated, and obviously in the last stages of a terminal illness. The young patient has a small, perfect bullet hole in his temple, as though the muzzle of the gun was placed right against his head. Blood has sprayed onto the opposite side of the pillow where the bullet came through in a mess of blood, bone, brain, and hair.

Dad's missing the left side of his face. His right eye is cloudy, staring at nothing. His glasses are on the floor next to his loafer, and one lens is cracked.

His hand is entwined with the hand of the young man.

I approach slowly, my mind not grasping what I am seeing. "Dad?" I touch his shoulder and know he's been gone for hours. There's no warmth under my touch, only cooling, stiffening flesh.

He'd come to the hospital this morning with the intention of mercifully helping this young man out of this terrible world. But in the end, he'd tried to protect his patient from the terror of dying at the hands of those soldiers.

I press my face against my father's shoulder, unmindful of the thickening blood under my sneakers. I breathe in the faint scent of his cologne and the smell of the laundry softener on his lab coat.

"This isn't real," I whisper.

Nick wraps his arms around me and holds me tightly against his chest. I feel his hot, damp tears against my cheek as they mix with my own.

CHAPTER 25

April 18
Nick

Cindy was broken.

We decided to stay until it starts to turn warm because her mental and physical state was too fragile following her father's death. She withdrew from me despite all I did to make her feel safe. She was broken and still is. But she's healing. I see the girl I've grown to love beginning to reemerge.

There's nothing here in Palmdale now. No military. Few survivors. And those who have survived are afraid and distrustful of each other.

We haven't banded together like in the movies. If anything, we've pulled apart, afraid of having to share or what the others will take.

Ben never told us where the cabin is located.

Going through my things the other night, I found a slip of paper with the name "Colin" scribbled on it, followed by an email address and an Instagram handle. It takes me a few moments of wondering before the light comes on, and I remember who exactly the mysterious "Colin" is.

The nerdy dude from the sporting goods store over at the Palmdale Mall. I hit him up a few times when the internet is getting a signal, but haven't gotten anything in return.

Until last night.

When his face flashes on the screen of my iPad, I question myself. Is this the same cat from the mall? He's extremely thin and looks much older. I assumed he was a college kid, but this guy looks like he could be thirty. Still, there's that shock of bright red hair that I remember.

"Colin?"

"Yeah." He doesn't appear to remember me, but the mention of Audrey and Cindy kickstarts things.

Long story short, we're picking him up in two days, and we're getting the hell out of here. Sure, it may not be smart. He could be a psychopath. But we're going to have to take that gamble.

We have to find other survivors out there. Ones who aren't paranoid and selfish. At some point, the world has to wake up and climb out of the dirt. We need to rebuild.

Maybe this time we'll get things right.

I don't want to come across as some kind of self-important asshole, but I'm sure nobody will ever see this besides myself. And I doubt I'll go back and reread it. Not much I want to relieve or remember about the past year, except for Cindy.

Cindy. For a while, I thought I'd lost her. The darkness in our lives had become so heavy that her eyes had lost their light. But losing a father (or a mother, or both) will do that to a kid. And we're still kids. For all the growing up we'd been forced to do since these things first started, we're still just kids.

I try not to think of the things we should be doing now. Getting ready for spring break, for graduation. For prom. For college. For getting out of Palmdale because we want to, not because we must get out.

I hear Cindy come inside. She's been out running. She begged me for one last run around the neighborhood. We usually go together—running has become a therapy for sorts for both of us. We've taken plenty of precautions against the Shamblers. A shovel behind one house, a pick axe behind the next. A baseball bat planted among a stand of overgrown shrubs. Usually, we don't need them, but sometimes a Shambler does show up.

Just to remind us why we're running.

Today, I stayed back to get everything in order one final time—making sure the M5 is still in good condition, then repacking. Colin claims to have supplies and food, as well. Just as long as he's able to pull his own weight, we'll be good.

I take a long look at Cindy and drink her in, more relieved that she's back than I let on. Her hair's coming out of its ponytail in wisps against her cheek, forehead, and neck. Her legs were slim and toned.

There's blood on the bottom edge of her shorts and the outside of her thigh. It's only a few drops, but I notice.

"How was your run?" I ask.

"It was good. A good run," she tells me, but then adds a little wink.

"Liar," I say. She'll tell me what happened later. Right now, it doesn't matter. She's with me and that's all that matters now. That's all that will ever matter.

She slips her arms around me and her lips brush mine, as soft as a feather. I breathe her in—the heady scent of her sweat, the spritz of jasmine body spray she's always worn on the back of her neck. For a moment, I'm taken back to that warm late summer day when in September. The only difference is the mud has been replaced with splatters of blood. And neither of us is so innocent anymore.

"I'm just glad I'm back," she whispers, before kissing me again.

"I am, too."

THE END...

?

DONNA BURGESS

Dive into the enigmatic world crafted by Donna Burgess, a masterful weaver of dark fiction and evocative poetry whose creativity extends far beyond the written word. A renaissance woman in her own right, Donna's passions are as diverse as her literary creations. When she's not conjuring chilling narratives or penning soul-stirring poetry, you can find her riding the crest of a wave, her heart in sync with the ocean's rhythm. An avid soccer player, she brings the same vigor to the field as she does to her storytelling, showcasing her dedication to both teamwork and individual prowess.

Her writing journey, spanning over two decades, has seen her work grace esteemed genre publications such as *Weird Tales, Horror Express, Chizine,* and many more.

Donna's academic pursuits are as impressive as her artistic ones. Holding a B.A. in Journalism and English, followed by an M.F.A. in Creative Writing, she has honed her craft with both precision and passion.

Visit her on the web: donnaburgess.com